no
love lost

kathy lee

Copyright © Kathy Lee 2007
First published 2007
ISBN 978 1 84427 252 5

Scripture Union
207–209 Queensway, Bletchley, Milton Keynes, MK2 2EB, England
Email: info@scriptureunion.org.uk
Website: www.scriptureunion.org.uk

Scripture Union Australia
Locked Bag 2, Central Coast Business Centre, NSW 2252
Website: www.scriptureunion.org.au

Scripture Union USA
PO Box 987, Valley Forge, PA 19482
Website: www.scriptureunion.org

The right of Kathy Lee to be identified as author of this work has been asserted by her in accordance with the Copyright, Designs and Patents Act 1988.

British Library Cataloguing-in-Publication Data.
A catalogue record of this book is available from the British Library.

Printed in the UK by CPI Bookmarque, Croydon, CR0 4TD

Cover design by Pink Cabana
Internal design and layout by Author & Publisher Services

✆ Scripture Union is an international Christian charity working with churches in more than 130 countries, providing resources to bring the good news about Jesus Christ to children, young people and families and to encourage them to develop spiritually through the Bible and prayer.

As well as our network of volunteers, staff and associates who run holidays, church-based events and school Christian groups, we produce a wide range of publications and support those who use our resources through training programmes.

Contents

1 A long, cold night 5

2 Machine guns .12

3 Home again .18

4 Carol singers 24

5 News report .31

6 Don't get involved 37

7 Decisions 43

8 Information received 49

9 An eye for an eye 56

10 Hospital visit 63

11 Dark alleys .71

12 The den 77

13 Near miss 84

14 Up in flames 91

15 Night shift .99

16 Grim and depressing 105

17 Evacuate! .113

18 Upwards .120

19 Battlefield .127

20 Shock waves 137

1

A long, cold night

'I can't believe I'm actually doing this,' said Charlie, as she packed her bag. 'Sleeping outside! In December!'

'It's for a good cause,' I reminded her.

'You should take some gloves and a hat,' said Emma. 'But you don't need to pack your entire make-up collection.'

'Oh yeah? If I turn blue with cold, I'm going to need it.' Charlie looked at me. 'You're lucky not to have that problem, Abena.'

I thought this was a dumb thing to say. OK, being African, I would never look blue with cold. But I would probably feel even colder than she did.

'Blue might suit you,' Emma said to her. 'Better than that pink eyeshadow, anyway.'

Charlie has to be careful which colours she wears, because of her ginger hair. She's small and skinny. Emma is taller – not as tall as me, though – with glasses and shoulder-length brown hair. The two of them are my best friends. We go to the same school and the same church.

We were getting ready for a sponsored sleepout in aid of homeless people in the UK and Africa. People from youth groups all over the city would be involved. We were allowed to take a sleeping bag, mat and pillow, but nothing else – not even a tent or a cardboard box.

The event was being held outside the cathedral. It was in Birton city centre, so lots of people would see us and perhaps donate some money... that is, if they could spare any from their Christmas shopping.

Charlie's mum dropped us off near the city centre, and we walked through the shopping centre. It was less than a month until Christmas. Bright lights, Christmas songs blaring out, plastic Santa Clauses everywhere... when I was younger, I would have started getting all excited. Now, at the age of 14, I couldn't work up that wide-eyed, expectant feeling any more. I must be getting old.

'What do you want for Christmas, Abena?' Emma asked me.

'I dunno. A surprise. I already know what I'm getting from my mum and dad – a new jacket. What do *you* want?'

She reeled off a long list of CDs and books and things. 'I know I won't get half of them, though. Mum and Dad keep telling me Christmas is far too commercialised. You know... the real meaning of Christmas is nothing to do with how many presents you get.' (You would expect Emma's parents to say that – after all, her dad's a vicar.) 'I tell them that's just an excuse for being mean with money.'

We turned a corner into Market Square. Above the stalls, with their tinsel and fairy lights, loomed the massive bulk of the cathedral. Pale searchlights cast dramatic shadows on the ancient stone walls. All it needed was a layer of snow to look exactly like a Christmas card.

But the crowd of people on the steps didn't belong on a Christmas card. With their coats, woolly hats and bundled sleeping bags, they looked more like an army of homeless people. One guy even had a dog on a string lead.

We met up with the people from our church youth group. Mark, one of the leaders, welcomed us, and Mary ticked us off on her list.

'Anyone want a collecting tin?' asked Mark. 'We ought to make the most of the time while there are still people in the market.'

The three of us took a tin and some publicity leaflets. We stood at the edge of the group, handing out leaflets and rattling the tin hopefully. Quite a lot of people gave us their loose change – after all, it was Christmas. And there had been news on the TV about the war in Mazundi, which had made so many people homeless.

Mazundi is the West African country where I was born. We left it when I was 4, but we've gone back since then to see my cousins. The last time was three years ago, when I was 11. After that the war began, and it wasn't safe to go back.

The war caused enormous problems. Thousands of people were driven from their homes when the rebels attacked or the army counter-attacked. They had to flee across the border into neighbouring countries, where huge refugee camps were set up. People got ill because of the crowded conditions, and children began to die of hunger. There was a worldwide appeal for money to ship in food and medical supplies.

Half the money we raised from our sleepout was going to Mazundi. The other half would be for projects in the UK, like the drop-in centre for homeless people which was starting up at our church. I was glad about this, because a few people didn't want to give to the African appeal.

'I don't see why we should send money abroad. Haven't we got enough homeless people in this country?'

'It's not our fault there are wars in Africa. Let the Africans sort out their own problems.' The woman gave me a hostile look as she said it. She obviously thought I should be back in Africa, not here in Birton asking for money.

'Charity begins at home, dear. What about those youngsters that sleep under the railway arches? They look like they need a good hot meal, I always think.'

To people like these – if they stayed around long enough – we explained that half the money was going to local projects. Sometimes that made them put their hands in their pockets. Most of them just walked away.

'Christmas spirit, or what?' Charlie muttered.

The market stalls were packing up and the shops were closing. But it was far too early to lie down for the night, especially when the ground would be freezing cold. We milled around, talking to people we knew and meeting a few new ones.

'Hey, Abena!' It was Mel, a girl I knew from school. 'There's a guy here that you should meet. He's from Mazundi. And I think he lives near you.'

I went over to join the crowd from her youth group. She led me towards a boy who looked about my age. 'His name's Danu. He's only been in England for a few weeks. Danu, this is Abena, the girl I told you about.'

Danu turned towards me with a welcoming smile. I liked the look of him – he had a lively face and a quick, energetic way of moving. He was the sort of person who gets noticed in a crowd.

But when he started speaking, I couldn't understand a word he said. And as he realised this, his smile faded.

He must belong to the Gwema tribe, from the north of Mazundi. My people were Zansi, from the south. The two tribes spoke different languages, and they had always hated each other. They were fighting on opposite sides in the war – in fact, it was the Gwema people who had started the whole thing by rebelling against the government.

I found I had taken a step backwards. 'I'm sorry, I don't understand,' I said stiffly. 'Do you speak English?'

'Yes. You are from the Zansi tribe, I think.

I nodded. 'And you must be a Gwema.'

There was a silence. Mel looked bewildered. 'But I thought... aren't you both from the same country?'

I said yes. Danu said no.

'That's what this whole war is about,' I explained. 'Don't you watch the news, Mel?'

'Yeah, sometimes, but I mean… I never really got my head round it. How can you be enemies if you belong to the same country?'

'My people want to be independent,' Danu told her. 'We do not want to be a part of Mazundi. We would like our own country, to rule ourselves.'

'And for that, thousands of people have to die?' I said angrily. 'Is it worth it?'

'My people were already dying! The president of Mazundi made himself rich by selling the copper from our land, but the men who worked in the mines were paid very little. They could not buy food for their children.'

'But the war has made things even worse!' I told him. 'Half a million refugees – women and children getting murdered – whole towns destroyed—'

'Destroyed, yes, by the government soldiers! Not by my people!'

I suddenly realised that we were both speaking loudly – shouting, almost. People were turning to look at us.

'OK, OK. Cool it, both of you.' It was Mark, the youth leader. 'We don't want another war breaking out right here. Do we?'

He led me back towards the St Jude's group. 'Do you know, Abena, that's probably the first time I've ever seen you get angry? You always seem such a calm person.'

'Yes, but he was saying…'

'Never mind what he was saying. Come and have some soup. It's going to be a long, cold night.'

2

Machine guns

We drank some soup from plastic cups, and listened to a band which had started playing on the steps of the cathedral. By now the air was freezing. The stars shone cold and white, like fragments of broken ice. Every breath turned to white smoke, and specks of frost sparkled on the pavement.

'We're going to be freezing tonight,' I said, shivering. 'Imagine what it will be like at 2 am.'

'You can always give up and go home if you feel really bad,' commented Emma, rubbing her hands together.

'Yeah, but then I won't get all the sponsor money.'

Charlie continued, 'It's easy for us. We can go home. I wonder what it's like to really be homeless?'

I guessed she was thinking about her brother, Zack, who had run away from home a few months before. She got a phone call from him every few weeks, so at least she knew he was still alive. The last she had heard, he was in Brighton.

'Have you heard any more from Zack?' I asked her.

'No. Mum thinks he might show up on Christmas Day. I told her not to get her hopes up.'

I often wished *my* brothers would leave home. It would be nice and peaceful without them. I have two brothers – one 16, one 11 – who argue all the time. I turn up my music to try and drown them out, and then Kwami does the same, and the neighbours bang on the wall, and Dad gets mad. If I were an only child, like Emma, life would be a lot calmer.

I knew that Kwami, my big brother, was somewhere around at the sleepout, but I didn't expect to see much of him. He had his own friends to hang out with. My little brother John was too young to take part – much to my relief. I seem to have spent half my life looking after John.

After a while the band stopped playing. They were replaced by a girl singer who wasn't up to much. She had a mournful, husky voice which made all her songs sound the same.

'I can't stand much more of this. Let's go for a walk around,' said Charlie. 'It might warm us up a bit.'

The square, empty of market stalls, was filling up with people. Most of them were involved in the sleepout. There was a large area marked out with traffic cones and tape, and plastic tarpaulins were being laid on the paving stones.

Round the edges there were a few groups of onlookers – boys who had been thrown out of pubs, and girls dressed up to go clubbing, and a drunk old woman who was trying to sing in competition with the girl with the microphone. (Perhaps she was the only genuine homeless person there.)

The boys watching didn't think much of the singers – professional or amateur. They swore at the old woman until she stumbled away into the darkness. Then they started heckling the girl singer.

'She's rubbish! Get her off!'

'Sing something decent, girl!'

'Do you do requests? Then sing *Silent Night* – silently.'

I could see a face I knew. It was a guy called Paul O'Farrell, who lived near us. All the O'Farrells were troublemakers – everyone knew that.

Paul, the eldest, was about 18, with close-cropped hair, thick eyebrows and a constant scowl. He couldn't hold down a job, yet he had an expensive-looking motorbike. He spent most of his time working on it, or riding around the estate late at night. Our elderly neighbour said it sounded worse than the fighter planes in the war.

When Paul slipped away from the crowd, I half-guessed what he was planning to do. All the same, I wasn't ready for the ear-splitting noise as he revved up his motorbike to full volume. The sound seemed to echo off the walls of the square, totally drowning out the voice of the singer. His friends looked like they were shouting and cheering – not that you could hear them, either.

Paul rode round and round in a circle, just beyond the traffic cones. It was illegal, because he was riding on the pavement in a pedestrian area, as well as probably being drunk. I could see several adults, including Mark, discussing what to do. One of them got a mobile out. Was he going to call the police?

'He shouldn't do that,' I muttered.

'What?' shouted Emma, her hands over her ears.

'He shouldn't call the police. It will only make Paul worse. Better to ignore him. He'll soon get bored, like a little kid, if no one pays him any attention.'

But a minute later, I saw a blue flashing light. (There are always lots of police around the city centre at night.) Paul saw it too. He gave a one-fingered salute and roared away down an alley, where no police car could follow him. The noise died away until it was lost in the distance.

'End of tonight's excitement,' said Charlie, and she gave a huge yawn.

Some people from our group had already unrolled their bedding. We seemed to have been allotted a space near the edge of the sleeping area, which would be colder than in the middle.

'Look on the bright side,' said Emma. 'If you have to get up in the night, you won't trip over so many people.'

'Anyone who trips over me is going to regret it,' remarked Charlie, wriggling into her sleeping bag. This wasn't easy because she was wearing so many layers of clothes.

'You look like a giant slug, squirming along,' said Emma.

'Oh, thanks a lot. You know, when you're homeless, that's when you find out who your real friends are.'

I lay down, feeling the cold strike upwards through the tarpaulin, mat and sleeping bag. I didn't think I would be able to sleep. Although the singing had stopped, the market place was still noisy. A taxi beeped; a burst of laughter and music escaped from a pub; and above it all, the cathedral clock chimed out, heavy and solemn as a funeral bell.

Trying to forget the cold, I thought about heat. It would be hot in Mazundi, even in December. I remembered how the heat used to hit us like a fist, as soon as we got off the plane. And I thought about the house where my cousins lived – a big house with a shady courtyard to keep off the sun. Small yellow lizards ran along the walls, and crickets chirped in the bushes. I loved that house.

My cousins were lucky. Their town hadn't been affected by the war... yet. But I'd seen on TV how whole towns had been reduced to rubble. Schools, churches, hospitals were sprayed with bullets. Dead bodies were left in the streets, with no one to bury them. All the survivors ran away, taking only the clothes on their backs.

I prayed, as I prayed every night, that peace would come soon, and that God would protect my family. Then, in spite of the cold, I must have drifted off to sleep.

Something woke me suddenly. Gunfire! Machine guns! I tried to sit up, totally confused about where I was. Darkness... cold... street lights... voices calling out...

'What's going on?' asked Charlie, sounding scared.

'It's that idiot on the motorbike. He's come back,' replied Emma.

Of course, that was what the noise was. Typical of Paul O'Farrell to come back and make a nuisance of himself! (No one tells the O'Farrells what to do.)

The noise tore the night apart as he gunned his engine. He roared around the sides of the square, waking everyone up. His helmet visor hid his face, but it was easy to guess he was laughing like mad. The time was 2 am.

Then he jumped the kerb and did a wheelie across the pedestrian area. But he hadn't allowed for the ice on the pavement. He skidded, lost control, tried to stop... skidded again...

Next moment, half a ton of motorbike was heading towards us. And we were lying right in its path!

3

Home again

I didn't scream. Instead, I prayed, 'Oh, God, help us!' And my prayer was answered – or else the rider was more skilful than he looked. He managed to get the bike under control again, almost like a rider reining in a horse. Amazingly, it slowed and came to a stop – just in time. The front wheel was almost on top of my sleeping bag.

I could smell oil and exhaust fumes. The roar of the engine hammered against my ears. For a long moment the rider held the bike quite still. Then he turned it around and rode away – more cautiously this time, though. He went off down a side street, and the engine noise died away into the night.

My friends crowded round. 'Are you all right, Abena?' asked Charlie.

'Yes. It didn't actually touch me.' I found that my voice was quite shaky, though.

Emma put her arm around me. 'That was scary. I really didn't think he was going to stop in time. I was praying like anything…'

'Me too.'

Mark and Mary came over to check that no one had been hurt. Most people were awake by now, although a few still snored on, undisturbed by the commotion.

'Did anyone get the number of the bike?' asked Mark.

'No, but I know who owns it,' answered Kwami, my brother. 'Paul O'Farrell. He lives near us.'

'How could you tell? He had a helmet on,' said Charlie.

'I know his motorbike,' Kwami replied, with a firm voice. 'And it's the sort of thing he would do. He's crazy!'

'We ought to report this to the police,' declared Mary. 'He could quite easily have killed someone.'

***

I didn't think I would ever get back to sleep that night. I lay on the ground, getting colder and colder. Even in the middle of the night there was traffic noise in the city, and now and then I thought I could hear motorbikes. When I closed my eyes I could still picture that bike, out of control, skidding straight towards me.

It was stupid to feel frightened, I told myself. Nothing had happened. I could have been killed... so? My parents had always told me there was no need to be afraid of dying. For someone who trusted Jesus, death was just the beginning of a new life in heaven.

More frightening was the thought that I might not have been killed – just horribly injured. A broken neck... paralysed for life. Or both legs totally crushed.

Then I thought of what Mum would say. 'What's the point of worrying about the past? You can't change it. And it's no use worrying about the future, because it's all in God's hands. Remember what the

Bible says, "I trust you to save me, Lord God, and I won't be afraid."'

Like comedians have catchphrases, Mum has words from the Bible for every occasion.

I trust you to save me, Lord God, and I won't be afraid. I tried to make that my catchphrase, too. Eventually I drifted off to sleep.

We were woken up by Mark and Mary, in time to hear the cathedral clock chiming seven. My body felt as cold and hard as the paving stones I'd been lying on. It took us ages to get out of our sleeping bags.

'Ohhhh…' Emma groaned, trying to get up. 'This is what it must feel like to be about 70.'

'No, this is what it feels like to be homeless,' said Mark. 'And we're lucky. We can go home and have a hot shower and turn the central heating up. Imagine what it's like to wake up like this every morning, all through the winter.'

Everyone was given a hot drink. Before we had finished, Emma's mum, who is always early for everything, arrived to pick us up. We were glad to see her.

'What about your brother, Abena?' she asked me. 'Would he like a lift? I think we can just about fit him in.'

'I'll ask him,' said Emma, before I could answer, and she hurried off to look for him.

Interesting… did Emma like my brother? Once or twice at youth group, I had noticed her looking at him. And he's quite good-looking, I suppose – but he doesn't have much confidence with girls. It's all because of a girl he went out with about a year ago. He was really keen on her, and she dumped him. Ever since then, he hasn't been out with anyone.

I didn't think Kwami would want to come back with us. I was wrong, though. Somehow we all squeezed into the little car, our sleeping bags on our laps. With the car's heating at full blast, we finally began to thaw out a little.

Emma's mum stopped outside the archway leading to Victory Court, where I live. Like a lot of people, she looked nervous at being in the neighbourhood. She probably thought the local kids would nick her hubcaps while she was still in the car.

Victory Court has got a bit of a reputation. It's an old, decrepit place, with windswept balconies, smelly stairwells and no lifts. In the centre is a rubbish-strewn courtyard where kids hang out, looking mean enough to mug their own grannies for a fiver. (But actually, when you know them, most of them are OK. It's just the odd idiot, like Paul O'Farrell, that you really have to look out for.)

Ever since we moved in, eight years ago, Mum and Dad have been trying to get a transfer to somewhere else. But no one wants to move here – or if they do, the place they're moving from is even worse.

I don't mind it too much. I'm used to it. What I don't like is the reaction I sometimes get when people find out where I live. I mean, not everyone from Victory Court is a danger to society.

At the moment – early on a Saturday morning – the place looked quite peaceful. Most people were still in bed. There was no one to see Kwami taking a close look at Paul's motorbike, which was chained up to a railing with a chain as thick as my arm.

'What are you doing?' I asked him.

'I just wanted to be sure it was Paul that nearly ran you over. And it was.'

'How can you be certain? All motorbikes look the same to me.'

'That's because you're a girl,' he said scornfully. 'Come on, I need some breakfast.'

We walked up the stairs and along the second-floor balcony to our flat. Old Mrs Hoskins, two doors along from us, was up already, polishing her brass letterbox.

'Been camping out?' she asked me, seeing my bedding roll. 'Bit chilly, isn't it, this time of year?'

I explained that it was a charity event, and she insisted on giving me some money – 50p out of a purse that looked almost empty. Mrs Hoskins was all right. Nosier than Sherlock Holmes, though – she knew all about everything that went on in Victory Court.

She said, 'What was your brother doing with that motorbike? Doesn't he know whose it is?'

'He does know.' I told her what had happened in the night.

'That Paul! He's not safe loose. He'll kill somebody one of these days. I'd report him myself, but…'

Her voice tailed off. I knew the reason for that. Anyone who annoyed the O'Farrells was likely to get a brick through their window, or dog pooh through the letterbox.

When we let ourselves into the flat, Mum had just got home from the night shift. (She's a nurse in the casualty department at Birton Royal.) She looked even more tired than I was.

'Was it a bad night, Mum?'

'Friday nights are always bad.' She sank down into a chair, too weary to take her coat off. 'It seems young people are getting more and more violent these days – getting into fights, using knives.'

'What happened?' Kwami was interested. 'Someone came in after a fight?'

'Three of them! Three boys, the same age as you. One of them lost a lot of blood – he nearly didn't make it.'

Dad said, 'Kwami, don't let me ever see you carrying a knife, all right?'

'Of course not,' replied Kwami. 'I'm not stupid.'

Dad had just got out of bed. Most of the time Mum works nights and Dad works in the daytime as a driver for a security firm. They sort of say hello and goodbye in the doorway as their paths cross.

Then my little brother John appeared, looking for his breakfast. And after that Mum crawled off to bed. I did the same – I felt as if I could sleep for a week.

Somehow I never got around to mentioning the motorbike incident to my parents. It seemed pointless. After all, no one had been hurt. I just wanted to forget the whole thing.

4

Carol singers

Although Mary had talked about contacting the police, nothing happened. I wasn't surprised. In Birton the police have worse things to worry about than a bit of dangerous driving. It might have been different if I'd actually been run over. 'Almost run over' didn't count for much.

But it wasn't long before I came across the O'Farrell family again.

I'd arranged to babysit for a family on the opposite side of the courtyard. The mum, Kim, was a single parent with two young girls. They were good kids, easy to look after.

When I arrived I noticed some badly spelt swear words sprayed on the door of Kim's flat. There's always graffiti in Victory Court, but not usually on people's front doors. Kim saw what I was looking at.

'The O'Farrell twins did it,' she said.

'Because you said something they didn't like?'

She scowled. 'All day they were playing *Knock Down Ginger* – you know, ring the doorbell and run away. I mean, I used to play that too as a kid, but I didn't keep on and on at it for ages. Anyway, after a bit I stopped answering the door – and then they did this.' She shrugged her shoulders as if to say it could have been worse.

I glanced along the balcony. It was obvious where the O'Farrells lived, a few doors along. Outside their flat was a small junk heap of motorbike parts, old toys and a broken chair. Every now and then the Council men would clear the rubbish away, but it soon mounted up again.

'Seems like they're worse than ever, now the latest boyfriend's moved out,' Kim said, letting me in. 'Him and Jackie had a massive row last week, and he left. So Jackie's drowning her sorrows in an ocean of vodka.'

Jackie was the O'Farrells' mum. She had four children. There was Paul, the mad biker; Robbie, who was in the year above me at school – except that he never went to school; and twin girls aged around 7. The twins seemed to have learned a lot from their big brothers, and would probably turn out even worse than they were. It was years since their dad had been around.

'Jackie doesn't seem to care what her kids do,' I said. 'No wonder they're out of control.'

'Yeah, yeah. The social workers always say you can't blame the kids, it's not their fault. But look at *my* kids. Their dad pushed off and left them, but that doesn't mean they behave like the O'Farrell brats, does it?'

'The O'Farrells should be on that *Bad Neighbours* programme on TV,' I said.

'You know what? They'd enjoy that,' said Kim. 'They would absolutely love it!'

After Kim had left, I watched TV for a while with her kids. They went to bed without any fuss. Feeling hungry, I put some bread in the toaster – Kim always told me to help myself to snacks. Then I went back to watching the film.

Next thing I knew, the smoke alarm in the hall was going off at full volume, and there was a horrible smell of burning. I ran into the kids' bedroom, shouting 'Fire! Quick, get up!'

The little girl, Kerry, sat up in bed, looking sleepy. 'That's not a fire, it's just the toaster.'

'Yes,' said Tara, her big sister. 'Didn't Mum tell you? The timer stopped working, but it still makes toast. You just have to watch it, that's all.'

In the kitchen, the toaster was smoking like a volcano. Bitter black fumes filled the room. I unplugged it, but that didn't stop the smoke alarm beeping away.

Tara marched into the kitchen and opened the fire door. She started wafting the smoke outside, quite calmly, as if this happened every day. 'Open the front door, too,' she said. 'Then we'll get like a wind blowing through.' More of a gale in fact, rushing through the flat from front to back!

In the end the smoke alarm stopped its angry beeping. I shut the front door, but, still detecting a slight whiff of burnt toast, I left the fire door open. It led to a narrow metal balcony along the back of the building, and a steep ladder going down. In a real fire, if you couldn't get out through the front door, this would be your way of escape. I was glad I hadn't had to get the two girls out that way – it looked almost as dangerous as an actual fire.

'OK, kids, back to bed. Do you think I should explain to the neighbours? They probably heard the alarm go off.'

'Nah, they're used to it,' replied Tara. 'It happens all the time. Can I stay up for a bit and watch the movie? I'm wide awake now.'

'All right then – just for two minutes.'

But the film had reached a boring stage. We both dozed off on the sofa until, some time later I was woken up by the doorbell. I could hear a couple of kids outside, singing the only carol that kids round here seem to know.

We wish you a merry Christmas
We wish you a merry Christmas
We wish you a merry Christmas
And a happy new year.
Good tidings la la
and la la la la
We wish you a merry Christmas
And a happy new year.

They knocked on the door this time. I tried to look out of the spy hole, but the children were too small to show up in it. So I opened the door on the chain.

Surprise, surprise! The singers were the O'Farrell twins, looking even scruffier than usual. They looked more like boys than girls, with their grubby faces, ragged jeans and uncombed hair. One of them – Tiffany? Chelsea? I never could tell them apart – was wearing a moth-eaten Santa hat. The other was holding out a plastic cup with a few coins in it.

What was their mum thinking of, letting them out on their own at this time of night? (Stupid question, she probably hadn't even noticed they'd gone.)

'You've got a nerve,' I said, 'expecting people to give you money after you spray-paint their door.'

'We never,' one said. 'It wasn't us,' the other chimed in.

They both spoke at once. Maybe it was true that twins could be telepathic.

I said, 'It was you all right. You were playing *Knock Down Ginger*, and when Kim wouldn't open the door, you sprayed it.'

'Who says?' said one, and 'I'll kill them!' said the other.

'Well, I'm not giving you anything,' I said.

The one with the cup shook the money under my nose. 'Aw, go on. It's Christmas,' she begged.

'And we ain't got no money to buy presents with,' said the other one.

Suddenly I felt sorry for them. They were probably going to have a lousy Christmas, unless their mum managed to sober up a bit.

'All right then, wait here a minute,' I said and began to close the door. Just as it shut, I saw a look of alarm on both their faces. Alarm? They ought to be pleased…

'Hold on,' one of them shouted. 'We ain't finished singing.'

'Yeah, come back!' The other one banged on the door.

I went to get some money from my jacket, which was in Kim's bedroom. But as I went in, my heart missed a beat. Something was moving in the semi-darkness. A dark figure crouched over the dressing table...

They heard me and whirled around. Next second they had barged past me, knocking me over.

'Hey! What do you think you're doing?' I shouted.

I got up and chased after the intruder into the kitchen, just in time to see the fire door slam shut behind them. For a few seconds I struggled with the handle, which was meant to be easy to open, but wasn't. (Tara must have been used to it.) This gave the intruder time to run along the balcony. Finally, I got the door open and leaned out to see the intruder banging on the fire door of another flat – no prizes for guessing which one.

Light from his kitchen window shone on his face, lean and mean and scarred. (Not knife scars, just bad acne.) It was instantly recognisable.

'Robbie O'Farrell!' I shouted. 'I saw you. I'm going to call the police.'

'What for? I ain't done nothing!' he shouted.

I was so angry, I set off after him. But then I stopped. I didn't like the narrow metal balcony, which shook slightly under my feet. I hated the darkness below – we were three floors up. This was not a good place to take on Robbie O'Farrell.

By now he'd managed to get into his flat. It was pointless for me to go any further. I turned back towards Kim's fire door, to see Tara looking out anxiously.

'What happened? Did someone get in – a burglar?'

'Don't be scared.' I tried to calm her down, although I wasn't exactly calm myself. 'It was only Robbie O'Farrell.'

'Did he take anything?'

'I don't know. We'll have a look in a minute.' But first I was careful to close the fire door securely.

Why on earth had I left it open? Even worse – I'd left it open and then gone to sleep. That was just asking for trouble. Oh help... if anything had been taken, it would be my fault.

We went into the girls' bedroom, where Kerry was sleeping peacefully. Nothing seemed to have been disturbed in there. In Kim's bedroom, a couple of drawers had been pulled out from her dressing table – that was all.

'Does your mum keep any money in here?' I asked Tara.

'She keeps her money in her bag, silly, not with her knickers.'

Maybe we had been lucky. It looked as if Robbie hadn't had time to do much. He must have got his kid sisters to knock on the front door, to distract my attention while he got in at the back. But actually, the twins had done me a favour – they woke me up. Without them, Robbie could have seen me asleep and calmly gone over the whole flat.

But it was no use thinking about it now – trying to put off the awful moment. I would have to ring Kim and give her the bad news.

5

News report

'It totally ruined Kim's evening,' I told Kwami later. 'She came rushing back home and checked through everything. But she doesn't think there's anything missing.'

'What is she going to do?' asked Kwami. 'Tell the police?'

'No. She says, what's the point? It will only annoy the O'Farrells – and she's got to live with them, three doors away.'

'Yeah!'

It was asking for trouble to get on the wrong side of the O'Farrells. Like the old man who tried to stop them playing football in the courtyard (where they had already broken the NO BALL GAMES notice with a well placed kick). He took their football away. In return he got nuisance phone calls, unwanted pizza deliveries, and superglue in his door lock. Soon after, he had a heart attack, brought on by all the stress. Well, that's one way of getting out of Victory Court.

'She should tell the police what Robbie did,' said John, my little brother. 'The O'Farrells think they can get away with anything. Someone needs to stop them.'

He was right, of course. But if I lived where Kim lived, I'd probably have made the same decision as she had. Just forget it. Nothing got stolen, so why cause trouble?

'Even if she did tell the police,' said Kwami, 'what would they do?'

'Lock him up,' said John.

'Don't be stupid,' replied Kwami. 'They don't lock up 15-year-olds.'

'Well, they ought to. When I'm Prime Minister, things are going to be different.'

'Hey, shut up a minute, you two,' I said anxiously, turning up the sound on the TV. It was a news item about the war in Mazundi, which had been going on for so long that it wasn't really news any more. After three years of it, the world had got bored. There were other, newer wars to report on.

'... when the Mazundi government troops retreated from Mbeka, centre of the copper-mining industry. Yesterday the rebel forces took over the area and drove triumphantly through the devastated streets. This is one step further in their campaign for independence,'

There were the usual pictures of the aftermath of fighting – ruined buildings, abandoned vehicles, and a convoy of jeeps driving through a storm cloud of dust.

'Today the town of Mbeka is eerily silent. It used to have a large population, mostly from the Gwema tribe, like the rebel army. Only a few are left, picking their way through the ruins, searching for food. The others may have fled the town when the fighting intensified. Or there may be a different explanation for the town's emptiness.'

Then the reporter paused for a second. There was a shot of a deserted street, with tattered flags hanging limp in the hot, still air. The only living creature was a stray dog, aimlessly wandering.

He went on, 'Rumours are reaching us that many people were killed by the government troops before they retreated. I believe there was a massacre here on an appalling scale. I have an eyewitness who claims to have seen hundreds of people being shot – men, women and children.'

The camera focussed on an old man, speaking in the Gwema language, with a voice-over translation into English. 'I saw the soldiers kill many, many people. The soldiers are Zansi. They hate the Gwema people.'

'Did you see what happened to the bodies of the people they killed?'

'They were buried in an old mine. Yes, children too, and babies. They killed them all.' He spread his hands wide, a gesture of helplessness which didn't need a translator. 'I was hiding. There was nothing I could do. I am an old man. If they found me, they would have killed me, too.'

'He's lying,' Kwami said angrily, switching off the TV. 'It's like Grandfather always said, "Never trust a snake, a scorpion or a Gwema."'

'But why? Why would the old man tell lies?' asked John.

'To make our people look bad, of course. To turn people against us. That news report will be seen all over the world.'

'It might be true, what he said.' I could still picture the old man's eyes, full of shock and outrage. 'After all, it's a war. Terrible things happen in wartime.'

'Maybe, but the rebels have done worse things to our people. Why don't the reporters talk about that? Because they are biased, that's why. It shouldn't be allowed!'

Kwami was getting quite worked up. That was because to him, Mazundi was home. He had been 7 years old when we left the country. Unlike me, he still remembered what it was like to live there, rather than just visit. He sometimes talked about going back for good, when things settled down.

But I was only four when we came to the UK. I couldn't remember living anywhere else. Although I had a Mazundi passport and could speak the Zansi language (at home we mostly spoke in Zansi), I didn't feel that Mazundi was my home. And yet Birton wasn't my home either.

Sometimes I felt I didn't belong anywhere.

***

At youth group on Sunday evening, the topic was forgiveness. Mark showed us a clip from a recent TV interview with a man who had been the victim of a terrorist bomb. He had been badly injured, and his small daughter had been killed, but he said publicly that he forgave the bomb makers.

'There's no point in being bitter,' he said. 'I could spend the rest of my life hating the people who did this, but that won't bring my daughter back. Every day I have to make the same choice over and over again – to hate or to forgive. It's better to forgive, like Jesus told us to.'

The interviewer asked, 'Do you mean you don't think the terrorists should be punished?'

'I didn't say that. If they are caught, they should go to prison like any other lawbreaker. But I don't want to waste my life on hating them and trying to get revenge on them.'

There was a lot of discussion about what he said. Harry objected, 'That's unrealistic. It's not human nature to forgive people who hurt you like that.'

'I agree with you, actually,' said Charlie. 'It's dead easy *talking* about forgiving people when they're not there. It's just words. But if he was face to face with his enemies, he would hate them all right.'

'Do you think so?' asked Mark, and he read out a verse from the Bible, where Jesus said:

You have heard people say, 'Love your neighbours and hate your enemies.' But I tell you to love your enemies and pray for anyone who mistreats you. Then you will be acting like your Father in heaven.

'That's what Jesus tells us to do. You're right, it's not easy. But it must be possible, or Jesus wouldn't have told us to do it.'

I thought to myself that it didn't really apply to me, because I had no enemies. I generally managed to get on all right with most people. My only real enemy recently – a girl called Rachel – wasn't around any more. Her family had moved her to a different school.

The very next day, the same verse came up in the booklet I use to help me read the Bible. (I try to read a bit from the Bible every day, although I don't always manage it.) Matthew chapter 5, verse 44: *But I tell you to love your enemies and pray for anyone who mistreats you...*

Perhaps God wanted to tell me something. I underlined the verse in my Bible. Maybe I ought to try and learn it by heart... but not right now. It was time for breakfast.

6

Don't get involved

On Wednesday – late night shopping night – I went Christmas shopping with Charlie and Emma. Coming back from the city centre, I was feeling quite pleased with myself. Most of the presents on my list had been ticked off.

It was nearly 9 o'clock when I got off the bus and said goodbye to my friends. I'd rung home to see if Dad could meet me at the bus stop. It would be just plain stupid to walk through Victory Court in the dark, on my own, loaded down with Christmas shopping. But Dad wasn't back from work yet and Mum had already left for her shift at the hospital.

Kwami reluctantly agreed to come and meet me, after I warned him that if I got mugged on the way home, he wouldn't be getting a Christmas present this year. It was raining, and by the time he reached me, he looked fed up. He was in the kind of mood where, whatever you said to him, he would only give one-word answers.

Trying to cheer him up a bit, I said, 'I know someone who likes you.'

He grunted something.

I said, 'She'd go out with you if you asked her.'

After a long pause, he said, 'Who?'

'Emma.' (I had finally got her to admit that, yes, she liked him, and no, she wouldn't mind if he asked her out.)

'Emma? Your friend? She's just a kid,' he said. 'How old is she?'

'Fourteen.'

'Just a kid,' he repeated, but I could see he was thinking about the idea. Emma's not bad looking now she's got rid of the terrible glasses she used to wear and got some funkier ones instead.

We walked on in silence. Up ahead of us, I noticed a guy on his own. When he came alongside the arched entrance to Victory Court, he hesitated. It looked as if he was trying to decide whether to go in or not.

There are two entrances on opposite sides of the courtyard, so in daytime people sometimes use Victory Court as a short cut from Canal Street through to Hill Street. Not many do that at night, though. They go the long way round.

But it was raining, and cold, and there seemed to be no one about. The lone figure made a decision – he went in. He vanished in the shadows of the archway. It's always dark under there because the lights have been vandalised and never mended.

A minute later it was our turn to enter the dark passageway. Near the far end, outlined against the orange glow of the lights in the courtyard, I saw two figures struggling together – fighting.

We both stopped instantly. There's an instinct that tells you: look out! Danger – don't go any closer!

I heard a cry of agony. Slowly, like a tree starting to topple, one of the fighters crumpled to the ground. The other one bent over him, then straightened up with something in his hand – a wallet?

He ran out into the courtyard. The sound of his footsteps faded in the distance.

A dreadful groan came echoing along the passageway. The fallen man struggled to his knees, then collapsed again. We looked at each other.

Don't get involved, said one voice in my head. *He needs your help,* said a different voice.

'Wait there,' said Kwami, going cautiously towards the victim. But I couldn't stand there alone in the dark – it felt safer to follow Kwami. He switched on the light on his mobile and shone it over the fallen man.

He wasn't a man. He was a young black guy, his face twisted in pain, his arms crossed over his chest. There was a dark stain on his jacket, a stain that grew bigger every second.

'He's been stabbed,' whispered Kwami. 'I'll call an ambulance.' He went into the courtyard, where the phone signal would be better, looking all around him as he went.

I knelt down beside the boy on the ground, wishing Mum was here. She would know what to do. I had no idea how to stop the bleeding. Oh God... help me!

Trying not to panic, I thought about what Mum would do. She would be talking to the guy, calming him down. 'It's all right,' I said, trying to sound confident. 'There's an ambulance on its way. You're going to be OK.'

The only answer was another groan.

'What's your name?'

'Danu Obindi,' he gasped.

Danu... where had I heard that name? Where had
I seen his face before? Oh, yes, of course... outside the
cathedral on the night of the sleepout. He was the boy
from the Gwema tribe.

Love your enemies looked like being my verse of
the week. OK, so he wasn't an enemy exactly – but
Kwami might think he was.

'Please... tell my mother,' whispered Danu.

'Your mother? Where is she?' When he didn't
answer I said, 'Danu! Talk to me! Where do you live?'

'Gordon House, Hill Street,' he managed to say.

'What number?'

I couldn't quite hear his answer: 15, or maybe 50. I
knew it would be better if he stayed conscious, so
I said, 'Who did this to you?'

No answer.

'Was he tall or short? Black or white? Danu! Tell
me!'

'Tall... White... Short hair,' he whispered.

His voice faded out. He was slipping into
unconsciousness; he must have lost a lot of blood. I
started doing what I should have done sooner –
praying for him. Please help him, God... please let the
ambulance come soon...

I was praying aloud. He must have heard me, for
his eyelids flickered open. 'Thank you,' he whispered.

And now I could hear the ambulance in the street.
Kwami ran to flag it down and lead the paramedics to
us. A minute later, a police car pulled up.

While Danu was put on a stretcher and lifted into
the ambulance, we told the police what we knew

about him – which wasn't much. 'He wanted us to tell his mother,' I said.

'It's all right. We can take care of that,' one of the policemen said. 'Did you see who did it?'

'Not really. It was too dark.' I told him what Danu had said about his attacker, and he wrote it down.

'What about you?' he said to Kwami.

Kwami shook his head. 'We didn't even see where he went. He ran off into the courtyard – that's all I know.'

Somehow, this didn't surprise the policeman. 'And how long ago would that have been?' he said rather wearily.

'I dunno. Ten minutes?'

'He'll be long gone by now,' said the other one.

They had a brief look around the courtyard. A few people, hearing the noise of sirens, had come out on their balconies, but most had stayed indoors. *Don't get involved* – it should be carved in stone above the entrance to Victory Court.

Soon the police went away. The ambulance had already left, with siren wailing. I picked up my scattered shopping bags. Seeing that the excitement was over, people turned back indoors – all except one.

Up on the third floor balcony, by the O'Farrells' flat, someone was still watching. He leaned on the rail, looking down at us as we crossed the courtyard and entered our stairwell.

'Paul O'Farrell,' I muttered to Kwami. 'It was him! He did it!'

'I'd say that would be a good bet,' agreed Kwami.

'It must be him, or why would he still be standing there, staring at us?'

'Yeah. And he probably saw us talking to the police. Does he think we grassed him up?'

In the shadows of the first floor landing, some boys we knew were having a smoke. (And when I say a smoke, I'm not talking about Silk Cut Purple.)

'Hey, Dexter, were you here earlier?' I asked. 'Did you see Paul O'Farrell run out across the yard?'

Dexter nodded. 'What's he done now?'

'Cut somebody,' said Kwami.

'So what's new?'

We left them in their haze of smoke. It would be no good trying to get Dexter and his friends to tell the police what they'd seen. The police were their enemies, and they weren't into *Love your enemy*.

When we came out on our balcony – second floor west – I glanced across to the far side of the courtyard. That dark figure was still there, silent and unmoving – still watching us.

It was like a threat: 'You'd better keep quiet. I know exactly where you live.'

7
Decisions

We were relieved to find that Dad was home. We told him everything that had happened.

His face turned serious. 'Why didn't you tell the police, if you knew who did it?' he asked.

'Because we didn't know – not then,' Kwami said. 'It was too dark to see him properly.'

'So you can't be sure,' he said.

'Some boys saw Paul running across the courtyard,' I said. (I didn't name names because Dad always told us to keep away from Dexter and his gang.) 'And then, just now, he was watching us from up by his flat – like really staring at us.'

'That still isn't proper proof,' Dad said.

From the doorway, John spoke up. 'If the police raided his flat, they might find evidence – like blood on Paul's clothes. Or even the knife. You should tell them!'

'You've been watching too much TV,' said Kwami. 'The police probably wouldn't listen to us. Remember when Robbie O'Farrell beat up that Polish kid? His parents reported it, but nothing happened.'

'Well, almost nothing,' I said. 'Robbie got cautioned.'

'He just laughed,' Kwami said bitterly.

'No one's doing anything to stop the O'Farrells,' John said, his voice rising in anger. 'What if they kill someone?'

I wondered if that had already happened. Was Danu still alive? Had he made it to the hospital? I wished there was some way of finding out, but I didn't even know which hospital he'd been taken to.

But I knew his address, I suddenly remembered. I could go round there, tomorrow or the next day, and ask about him.

Kwami said to Dad, 'It seems to me you don't want us to tell the police. Why not?'

Dad hesitated. 'For one thing, you are not absolutely certain it was Paul, are you? And then, how will he react if you report him?'

'I'll do it! I'm not scared!' said John.

Dad gave him one of his looks. 'John, you should be in bed. Go on – now!'

Reluctantly, John went out into the passage. I waited for the sound of his bedroom door closing, but didn't hear it.

'I said GO TO BED!' Dad roared, and John scuttled into his room.

I remember when the sound of Dad's voice used to have that effect on me, too. When I was younger, I thought Dad was the best and bravest man in the entire world. If he praised me, I felt wonderful. If he told me off, I wanted to hide under my bed.

Was Dad afraid of what might happen if we reported Paul O'Farrell? I certainly was. But somehow I'd expected Dad to be braver than that.

'What do you think we should do?' I asked him.

'I think the right thing is probably to tell the police,' he said. His face was troubled. 'But I also think that by telling them, we may get into danger. And I don't want us to risk that.'

'Dad, you always said to do the right thing and God will protect you,' I said.

'Yes. I've always believed that. But...' His voice trailed off.

'But what, Dad?'

'I had some bad news recently. That's all.' His voice was flat.

'What bad news?' asked Kwami.

'I don't want to talk about it. But I've learned that doing the right thing – or what you believe is the right thing – sometimes has a terrible ending.'

His eyes seemed fixed on somewhere far away, beyond the kitchen wall, beyond the courtyard, far out into the night.

***

'What was he talking about?' I asked Mum the next day, after school. She was cooking some fish stew for us to eat before she went off to do the night shift.

'It's about a friend back home. His best friend from childhood – Erasto. He grew up to be a church minister, and we went to his church the last time we were in Mazundi. Do you remember?'

Yes, I remembered. The church service was much livelier than at St Jude's, with wonderful singing and a lot of dancing. Sometimes people would start up a song right in the middle of the sermon, but the pastor just smiled and joined in.

'Well, Erasto spoke out against some of the bad things that are happening in Mazundi.'

'The war, you mean.'

'Not only the war. Everyone says that the last elections were fixed, so that President Baretse didn't get voted out. The President is very rich. A lot of money that should be spent on hospitals and schools and so on, is being spent on the President's new palace. And also on the army, and the people who keep him in power.'

It wasn't the first time I had heard this. My parents, when they got letters or phone calls from our cousins, often talked about it. Sometimes they said that the President must be mad – still desperately clinging to power, with the country disintegrating around him.

Mum went on, 'Erasto was brave enough to speak out against the President. He knew it was dangerous, but he believed God had told him to do it. And he wrote to everyone he knew. He said, "If good men do nothing, evil men will triumph."'

Now I could guess what Dad had been talking about. 'What happened to him?'

'He was arrested by the police… the President's police. Three days later his wife had to go and identify his body. He had been tortured so terribly that he must have been glad to die.'

No wonder Dad had been upset. His friend had done what he thought was right – what God wanted him to do – but God had not protected him. He had died an agonising death.

There was something here that didn't add up. I'd always been taught that God was in control of everything. He was powerful and strong, and he loved us, his children, like a father. Surely he could have stopped Erasto's enemies from killing him.

'Mum,' I said, 'why do you think God let that happen?'

She looked at me. 'I've been asking myself that question, too. But you know, God's children don't always get to live a calm, peaceful life. Look at Paul in the Bible – he was put in prison, and beaten, and stoned, and almost drowned. But he wrote that it made him happy to share in the sufferings of Jesus.'

I said nothing. I couldn't imagine being happy to be imprisoned and beaten.

'And whatever we go through in this life,' Mum went on, 'it won't matter when we get to heaven and see the glory of God. That's where Erasto is now. He's in the place where there is no more pain and suffering – only joy.'

'Does Dad believe that?' I asked.

'Yes, of course. He's upset, though, because he's lost his friend.'

It was more than that, I thought. Perhaps Dad felt that he couldn't trust in God the way he used to. God had let him down.

All very confusing, and meanwhile, we still had to decide what to do. Tell the police about Paul O'Farrell, or keep quiet? Take the safe path, or risk making an enemy – a whole family of enemies?

When Dad came home, we had a family conference around the kitchen table.

Mum said, 'I just had an idea. There's that help line you can ring up – *Crimefighters*, or something, it's called. They don't make people give their names if they don't want to.'

'Good idea,' said John. 'Ring them up, Kwami.'

'I bet Paul will still think it was us who reported him,' Kwami said to me. 'He saw us talking to the police, remember?'

I replied, 'Yeah, but nothing's happened since then. I mean, they haven't come after him. Like, if we'd told them his name, they'd have arrested him by now.'

'We could ring that number tomorrow,' said Kwami. 'What do you think, Dad?'

Normally Dad would have told us what he thought at the very start, and made sure we all listened. This time, he'd said nothing at all.

'I don't know,' he said. 'I have a bad feeling about this. But if we keep quiet, and Paul attacks someone else...'

'You'll feel even worse,' said Mum.

She served out the food. Normally I love fish stew the way Mum makes it, with okra and ginger. That night I could hardly eat any. John made up for it by eating his own share and mine too.

'So, are you going to call that number?' he asked Kwami.

'I don't know!' Kwami pushed his plate away. 'Shut up, will you? It's nothing to do with you.'

He was wrong there – as we soon found out.

8

Information received

By next morning the decision was made, and Kwami rang the helpline. He used his mobile and withheld the number, because he thought it would be harder to trace where the call had come from.

I listened to his end of the conversation, as he described what had happened, and gave Paul O'Farrell's name and address. It all seemed quite simple. He didn't have to answer any awkward questions, and when he rang off, he was smiling with relief.

I felt relieved too. It was out of our hands now.

John said, 'What will happen? Did they tell you?'

'They said they'll pass the information on to the police.'

'You should have rung them sooner,' John went on. 'Paul's had enough time to get rid of the evidence.'

Perhaps he was right. It was now 36 hours since the attack. Paul could easily have thrown his knife in the canal, and washed any blood off his clothes.

'The police use DNA nowadays,' said Kwami.

'What is DNA, exactly?' I asked.

'It's science,' Kwami said vaguely. I could tell he didn't know what it was, any more than I did. 'They can prove anything with DNA.'

John said, 'DNA is in every cell of your body, even hairs and nail clippings. So the police can tell if—'

'Oh, shut up!' Kwami pushed him off the sofa.

People often say that John is the clever one of the family. Kwami hates that. Even at the age of 11, John sometimes wins their arguments. Not their fights, though. Kwami always wins the fights.

***

I still didn't know what had happened to Danu. So, on the way back from school, I made a detour along Hill Street, looking for Gordon House. It turned out to be a big old house which had been turned into some kind of hostel, run by the Council.

I rang the bell numbered 15, outside the front door. At first I thought no one would answer. Then a nervous voice came from the intercom.

'Yes? Who is there?'

'Is this where Danu lives?'

'Who is this?' The voice sounded even more afraid.

'I was there when he got attacked. It was my brother who called the ambulance. I just wanted to find out if Danu is OK. Is he still in hospital?'

'Yes, he is. Come in, please. We are upstairs.'

A buzzer rang, letting me open the front door. The dim-lit hall was filled with a mixture of sickly smells – chip fat and curry spices and sour milk. I went up some grubby stairs onto a dark, dismal landing, with several doors, one of them open.

Inside it stood an anxious looking woman. She wore traditional Mazundi clothes in a vivid pattern of orange and yellow – bright and cheerful, totally unlike her face.

'Are you Danu's mother?' I asked. 'Is he all right?'

'He is in the Winfield Hospital. The doctors say that he almost died. The knife went very near to his heart. But now they say that he will live… they hope.'

'Have you been to see him?'

'I went yesterday. But he was asleep. I will try to go tomorrow. It's difficult… the children.'

I looked down and saw two young children clinging to her legs. I smiled at one of them. He hid his face in her dress.

She said, 'Yesterday, I left them with my neighbour. But today she is not here. And they cannot walk as far as the hospital.'

'You could get a bus,' I suggested. 'Number 33 – it goes right past the hospital.'

She said nothing, and I wondered if money was a problem. Or perhaps she didn't want the kids to see their big brother lying there, seriously injured.

'You know, I could look after the children for you,' I said on an impulse. 'I often look after kids. I'm quite good with them.'

Again she was silent. Her eyes searched my face. I could guess how much she longed to see Danu, and yet she knew nothing about me – I was a complete stranger. (A stranger from the tribe of her enemies… but I wasn't about to tell her that.)

'Danu wanted to see you,' I said. 'When I was with him, waiting for the ambulance, he said, *Tell my mother*. That's how I knew where you live.'

Suddenly she decided to trust me. 'Come in,' she said.

The big, high-ceilinged room had an empty look. There were bunk beds, an ancient sofa bed, a couple of chairs, and in the corner a sink and a small cooker. But no children's toys, no TV, no possessions at all, really. Perhaps the family had arrived in the UK with only what they could carry in a suitcase, and they hadn't the money to buy any non-essential things.

Danu's mum started talking to her children in their own language. I could guess what she was telling them, by the way they turned round to look at me. Then she put on her coat.

'Thank you,' she said to me. 'I will come back quickly.' And she was gone.

At once the little girl, who looked about two years old, started to cry. You couldn't really blame her. Mamma had vanished, and in her place was a complete stranger. I tried to pick her up and comfort her, but she fought me off, hitting me with her tiny fists and screaming louder. Her brother stood quite still, staring at me with terrified eyes.

Oh, help! I couldn't use any of the normal methods of calming children. I didn't speak their language; they were too young to have learned English at school. And there were no toys or books to distract their attention.

Toys! I had a sudden inspiration. I rang home. It was John who answered, because Mum was still in bed. I asked him to bring around the box of old toys that we keep for visiting kids to play with.

'Aw, do I have to? I'm watching TV.'

'It won't take you long. I'm only around the corner.'

Five minutes later he rang the bell. I almost didn't hear him, because the little girl was still screaming. I let him in; he handed over the box of toys, then made a quick exit, covering his ears.

But the toys had a magic effect. As soon as I started taking them out of the box, the little boy was interested. I gave him some toy cars to play with. Then I found a quacking duck to pull along on a string, and his sister stopped crying to stare at it.

By the time their mother came back, the two of them were playing quite happily. I had already decided to leave the toys with them, as long as my mum didn't mind. But when I had tried to ring home, there was no answer – which was strange. Normally, by now, Mum would be up, getting ready for the night shift.

'How is Danu?' I asked his mother.

'He is awake. He talked to me. He was happy to see me,' she said, smiling. 'Now I think that the doctor is right – Danu will not die. Thank you for helping me.'

'Do you know how long they'll keep him in hospital?' I asked.

'No, they did not tell me.'

I gave her my phone number, so that she could call me if she wanted my help again. 'Would it be all right if I went to visit Danu, too?' I asked. 'Maybe in a few days?'

'Oh yes, please go. He is in Ward C at Winfield Hospital. He does not have many friends here. We are new in England.'

'Are you here because of the war in Mazundi?' I asked, adding hastily, 'I saw it on TV.'

'Yes. We thought we would be safe here...'

It was crazy. They'd escaped from a war-torn country, only for Danu to get stabbed here, in so-called peaceful England.

Danu's mother invited me to stay and eat with her family. But I had already seen how little food they had on the shelf, and I didn't want to deprive them.

'Thanks, but my mum will be expecting me back,' I said, looking at my watch – it was 6.30. I just hoped John had remembered to tell Mum what I was doing, when she woke up.

It was dark by now. Going through the archway into Victory Court, I couldn't help shivering slightly. This was where Danu had been attacked... But everything was quiet.

I went up the stairs and along the balcony. Before I reached our flat, another door opened abruptly, making me jump.

'Abena! Wait a mo!'

It was old Mrs Hoskins. She said, 'I'm glad I caught you. Your mum asked me to give you a message. She's had to take your little brother to hospital.'

'What?'

'Yes, he got beaten up. She thinks he has a broken rib. It was one of *that* lot that did it.' And her eyes turned towards the flats on the opposite side of the court.

'You mean the O'Farrells?'

'Who else, love?'

'Oh no! When did it happen?'

'About half past four.'

John must have been on his way back from the Hill Street hostel. I felt terrible. If he'd stayed at home, this wouldn't have happened.

'He'll be all right, love.' Mrs Hoskins patted my arm. 'Don't you worry. Luckily your big brother was on his way home, just at the right time. He's bigger than Robbie O'Farrell. He soon saw him off.'

'It was Robbie, was it?' I said, surprised. 'I thought it might have been Paul.'

'Oh no, haven't you heard? Paul's been arrested. The police came this afternoon, and arrested him, and took him away.'

9

An eye for an eye

Mrs Hoskins told me everything she knew about Paul's arrest – which wasn't much.

'The first I knew was, I heard a kerfuffle outside, and I went to have a look. There was three coppers on the balcony up there, taking Paul away, and his mother was trying to stop them. Shouting and rampaging, she was – effing and blinding all over the place. Drunk as a fiddler, I reckon. Any minute now, they'll arrest her too, I thought.'

'But they didn't?'

'No, they seemed to think one O'Farrell at a time was enough to cope with. I can't say I blame them.'

'Was Robbie there while this was going on?' I asked.

'I don't know, love. But he must have heard about it soon enough. The news was all around the Court in five minutes. And everyone says Paul deserves it. There's no love lost between the O'Farrells and the rest of Victory Court.'

***

Robbie had attacked John to try to get back at us for Paul's arrest. I was sure of it. He wasn't brave enough to take on Kwami, who was bigger and stronger than him, so he beat up an 11-year-old kid.

What would have happened if Kwami hadn't come along at the right time? Thank God he did, or John could have ended up with worse than a broken rib. Robbie could have kicked his head in.

I tried to ring Mum, but couldn't get through. Of course, if she was at the hospital, her mobile would be turned off.

There was no one at home. Kwami was out and Dad wasn't home from work yet. I walked restlessly around the flat, getting more and more angry. Something should be done about that family! They didn't deserve to live among ordinary, law-abiding people! The Council should rehouse them on a desert island and let them destroy each other!

At last the phone rang. It was Mum.

'Oh, Mum! Is John all right?'

'Yes, he is, thank God! They say he hasn't broken anything. Of course, he's a bit shaken up, and so am I. We'll be home in half an hour. Could you start getting the supper ready?'

Feeling guilty – I should have thought of doing that without being asked – I went into the kitchen. Mum had started cutting up some chicken and then abandoned it. I decided to cook it with some peanut butter and garbanzo beans. Before I'd got very far, I heard the front door open.

It was Kwami, all on his own.

'Where have you been?' I asked him.

'Hunting down Robbie O'Farrell,' he replied. 'Dexter told me where to find him – in the basement. He's got like a den down there. I found him and I sorted him out.' Kwami smiled – a fierce smile with no laughter in it, like the grin of a skull.

'What do you mean – sorted him out?'

'I mean taught him a lesson. Made sure he leaves my little brother alone. I showed him all right!' He waved his fist in the air. To my horror, I saw there was blood on the sleeve of his jacket.

'Kwami! What did you do to him?'

He laughed then. 'I didn't kill him, if that's what you're thinking. I just roughed him up a bit.'

'But the blood...'

'That was his nose. I think maybe he's got a broken nose. That's fair, isn't it? – a broken nose for a broken rib. Like an eye for an eye, a tooth for a tooth.'

My first instinct was to feel glad. Robbie had asked for it – he deserved everything he got. But then I started thinking.

'Robbie won't take this lying down,' I said. 'He'll try to get back at you somehow.'

'He won't dare.'

'Yeah, maybe he won't dare attack *you*. But what about John, or me? Or even Mum? You shouldn't have done it, Kwami.'

'You think we should just let Robbie get away with what he did to John?' He was angry now. 'Well, I don't. He's got away with far too much already. That's why he behaves the way he does – because he never gets punished. I bet Dad thinks I did the right thing.'

'I bet Mum doesn't.'

***

We were both right. Dad was on Kwami's side; Mum agreed with me. As for John, he was really pleased when he heard what Kwami had done. He seemed to realise that in spite of all the arguments between the two of them, his big brother cared about him. (Well, sometimes anyway.)

He showed off his injuries quite proudly – a cut lip which was swelling up horribly, a bloodshot eye, and several sore ribs. An X-ray at the hospital had proved that no bones were broken. But he'd been told to rest for several days. As it was less than a week until the end of term, his Christmas holidays had started early.

'It will be safer if you stay at home,' Mum told him. 'I don't want you going out there and running into Robbie again. And what about you, Abena? Don't come home from school on your own – promise me.'

'I never do, Mum. I always walk home with Charlie and Emma.'

Kwami said, 'I could wait for you after school and walk home with you. Just in case…'

I was about to say that wasn't necessary, when I remembered that Emma might rather like the idea of Kwami walking home with us. 'OK,' I said.

Suddenly there was a loud ring of the doorbell. Not an ordinary ring – it went on and on, like a fire alarm. And someone was banging on the door.

Cautiously, Dad looked out through the spy hole. 'It's the O'Farrell woman.'

'Don't open the door,' said Mum.

The ringing continued. Then it stopped, and the shouting began.

'I know youse are in there! Come out, you cowards! Look what your son did to my boy. I'll report him, so I will!'

I looked cautiously out of the window. It was dark outside, but the light on the balcony showed two people outside our door – Robbie and his mum.

Jackie O'Farrell was a big, untidy-looking woman, with brassy blonde hair, dark at the roots. Her too-tight jumper, which had food stains down the front, showed every bulge of her fat body. Anger made her face look even uglier than usual.

Robbie was lurking behind her. He had a huge piece of sticking plaster over his nose. He looked as if he'd been dragged along by his mum and didn't really want to be there. One arm was down by his side, carrying something – something heavy, by the look of it.

'Abena, come away from the window,' Mum said. 'And close the curtains.'

The curtains wouldn't be much protection, I thought, if Robbie was about to throw rocks at our window.

Jackie was still shouting, swearing, and banging on the door. I won't even try to write down what she said, because most of it was racist and all of it was full of hatred. It made me feel sick, listening to her. I tried to block my ears, but I couldn't.

'Will she really report Kwami to the police?' John whispered.

Kwami, for the first time, began to look uneasy. He had never been in trouble with the police up to now.

If he did get a police record, it might mess up his life. There are lots of jobs you can't even apply for if you have a record.

'Dad, tell her Robbie started it,' I said. 'Tell her what he did to John.'

'No, don't say anything,' Mum begged. 'The woman is drunk. It will only make her angrier.'

Dad stood there for a long minute, making up his mind. Perhaps he was praying. Then he opened the door. Jackie was so surprised, she stopped in mid-screech.

'If you report my son to the police, I will report *your* son,' he said. His voice was quite calm. 'You may not know this, but it was Robbie who started this. He beat up my younger son so badly that he ended up in Casualty. Come here, John.' And he showed Jackie the injuries to John's face.

Jackie gaped at him. Then she turned to Robbie. 'Is that true?'

Robbie muttered something. His mum swore at him and whacked him on the side of the head. He staggered sideways – she probably weighed twice as much as he did. The thing he was carrying fell with a solid-sounding thud.

'You stupid idiot!' she yelled at him. 'You want to end up like Paul, do you? It won't be a caution they give you this time! Gerrout. Gerrout of my sight.'

Robbie made off towards the stairs, with his mother lurching after him. We all looked at each other. I was so relieved, my knees felt weak.

Kwami went out and picked up what looked like a fragment of broken wall – two bricks cemented together. This was what Robbie had been carrying.

'He was going to chuck this through the window,' he said.

'You'd never be able to prove that,' I said.

'Oh yeah?' said Kwami. 'Why else would he carry it here? Just taking the wall for a walk?'

For some reason this made everyone collapse with laughter. Everyone except Mum, who was busy getting ready to go out again, back to the hospital to work the night shift. She hadn't even had time to eat.

Dad went out with her to make sure she got safely to the car. The car park at the side of the building was pretty dark – just the sort of place where enemies could hide, unseen. But Robbie wouldn't dare to take on my Dad. I loved the way Dad had stood there in the doorway, strong and immovable, protecting us all.

When he hadn't come back ten minutes later, I began to worry. I went to the door to look out for him. He was just coming along the balcony, and his face was grim.

'The car has got four flat tyres,' he said. 'Your mother had to call a taxi.'

'*Four* flat tyres?'

'Yes. It looks like someone stuck a knife in them. And the O'Farrell twins were sitting on the wall, watching us, laughing their heads off.'

10
Hospital visit

'Kwami said, an eye for an eye and a tooth for a tooth,' I told Emma. 'He said it's in the Bible. Is he right?' If anyone knew the answer, Emma would. After all, her dad is our vicar.

'I'm not sure, but I can find out,' she said. She fetched a big, fat book from her dad's study. She said it was a concordance – a sort of index to the Bible – and she started looking up the word *tooth*. Then she said, 'Try Exodus chapter 21, verses 23 to 25.'

I looked it up in her Bible.

The payment will be life for life, eye for eye, tooth for tooth, hand for hand, foot for foot, burn for burn, cut for cut, and bruise for bruise.

'Is that really in the Bible?' said Charlie. 'It sounds kind of… savage. And you know what they say. An eye for an eye, a tooth for a tooth – after a while the whole world ends up blind and toothless.'

I saw what she meant. Robbie beat up John, so Kwami beat up Robbie, so Robbie planned to put a brick through our window, and his sisters attacked our car… It could go on forever, if we let it.

'Hang on a sec,' said Emma. She was still looking at the big book. 'There's another reference mentioned – Matthew 5, verses 38 and 39.'

It was in the middle of the *Sermon on the Mount*, where Jesus talked to his followers about how they should live.

You know that you have been taught, 'An eye for an eye and a tooth for a tooth.' But I tell you not to try to get even with a person who has done something to you. When someone slaps your right cheek, turn and let that person slap your other cheek.

'What?' said Charlie. 'That can't be right. Read it again.'

I read it again. The words weren't new to me; I must have heard them in church before this, or read them in the Bible. In those days, when I had no enemies to speak of, the command was easy to hear and well, forget about. But now...

Charlie said, 'So thieves and muggers and murderers shouldn't be punished? That's just stupid. We need to have laws and punishments. Otherwise, the thieves and murderers will keep on doing it. They'll take over the entire world.'

Emma said thoughtfully, 'Punishment isn't the same as revenge. Revenge is what Jesus was talking about. *Do not try to get even with a person who has done something to you.*'

I remembered Kwami's face when he came in after beating up Robbie – his fierce, triumphant smile, his pride in what he'd done. It wasn't punishment that he'd been dishing out. It was revenge.

As for the O'Farrells, they loved revenge. They specialised in it. Like when a neighbour complained to the Council about their noise, which was keeping her baby awake. For weeks after that, they would ring her doorbell at three in the morning.

I wondered if they felt they had paid us back yet. Revenge on revenge… when would it ever stop?

***

It was Saturday, the day after all the fighting. I was at Emma's house, getting ready to go on a mission. We had volunteered to give out flyers about the new project at St Jude's – a drop-in centre for homeless people. Today was the first day that the church hall would be open for anyone who needed it. There would be hot food, a cup of tea, and shelter from the biting cold.

In the church hall a few other volunteers from the youth group had gathered together. Mark gave us each some leaflets to hand out, and told us which areas to go to. As we stepped outside I wrapped my scarf tighter around me. Oh, it was cold! Perhaps I shouldn't complain about living in Victory Court – at least I had a home to go to and a warm bed at night.

Charlie, Emma and I went down to the industrial estate, where people often slept rough under the railway arches. On a piece of waste ground there was a fire burning in a metal container, with a couple of old men huddled beside it. Rather nervously, we went up to them and gave them a leaflet each.

'What's this?' one said suspiciously, staring at it with red-rimmed eyes.

'I can't read this. Lost my glasses,' said the other.

Emma explained what it was about. They didn't seem too impressed.

'We're all right here, we are,' the first one mumbled. 'Got a nice fire going. It'll go out if we leave it.'

'OK,' Charlie said. 'But remember, if you do want to come to the centre, it's open twice a week – Thursday and Saturday. It'll be open on Christmas Day, too.'

'What's today, then? When's Christmas?'

'Er… it's Saturday today,' I said, 'and Christmas is a week on Monday.' After all, if you were homeless and jobless, it wouldn't be surprising to lose track of what day it was.

'Christmas!' the first man swore and spat on the ground. 'Christmas! Load of claptrap. Everybody would be nice to each other one day a year. What about all the other days, eh?'

There was no answer to that. 'Yes, well… bye then.'

We met a few other people: a teenage girl with the dead-looking eyes of a druggie; a mad old lady with all her belongings in a shopping trolley, who assured us that she wasn't homeless, saying, 'I've got a lovely home, dear, if only I could remember where it is.'

It was dawning on me that not all homeless people needed or wanted a day centre to visit. But there were a few people who sounded interested, and took a leaflet, and even asked for directions to St Jude's. Maybe we weren't totally wasting our time.

By early afternoon we had covered the area that Mark had assigned to us, and we were so cold that Charlie was checking her fingers for the first signs of frostbite. It was time to head back. But then I saw a sign: WINGFIELD HOSPITAL.

This was where Danu was, unless they'd sent him home. On an impulse, I decided to go and see. I told the others I would meet them back at Charlie's place.

***

I'd already decided that if Danu's mother was there, I would just say a quick hello and goodbye. Almost everyone else in Ward C seemed to have visitors. But Danu was sitting by himself in the day room, staring at a TV with the sound turned down.

The first time I ever met him I thought he was quick moving, full of energy and life. Now he sat quite still in an armchair, with two pillows propping him up. He was wearing slippers and a dressing gown, like an old grandad.

One thing hadn't changed, though – that smile of his. When he saw me coming towards him, the smile lit his whole face.

'You are the one who helped me!' he said. 'Thank you. I think, without you, I would be dead now.'

'It wasn't just me,' I said, embarrassed. 'My brother went to help you first, and he rang for an ambulance.'

'Yes, but you were with me. You prayed for my life. You would not let go of me.' His eyes, deep and intense, held me so that I couldn't look away.

I sat down beside him and asked how he was feeling. He said that the knife wound didn't hurt him too much as long as he sat still. When he tried to move, it was like being stabbed again.

'I was foolish,' he said. 'I tried to fight the robber. I did not want him to take my money. But he had a knife.'

'Did you get a good look at him?' I asked.

'The police have asked me this. They showed me some pictures, but I don't know if one of them is the robber. It happened quickly, and it was night. And you? Did you see him?'

'I know who he was – he lives near us. The police arrested him yesterday.'

'That's good. Now he will not hurt anyone else.'

I told him a bit about what had been happening, and he listened intently. He seemed to have forgotten our very first meeting, when we discovered that our people were enemies. And now there was a bond between us, a bond stronger than family or tribe – I had helped to save his life.

Although I have two brothers, I sometimes feel shy and awkward around boys – but not with Danu. He was easy to talk to, and after a while I felt as if I'd known him for ages.

He told me about his father, who was still in Mazundi, in great danger. He was a writer who had tried to protest against the corrupt evil President Baretse. His books had been banned and he had gone into hiding, knowing that if he was caught by the President's men, he would face certain death.

His family was in danger too, as long as they stayed in Mazundi. Some friends had got together enough money for them to leave the country.

'I did not want to leave Mazundi,' said Danu. 'I wanted to stay. My father stayed! He did not run away! But he told me, "Danu, you have to go. You must look after our family. When it is safe, bring them back."'

'He thought you would be safe here,' I said. 'But he was wrong.'

'Yes. And who will look after my family now?'

His face was anxious. I wondered what it felt like to have to be the man of the family at the age of 14.

'Don't worry. You'll soon be out of hospital,' I said, and hoped that it was true. 'But in the meantime, I could ask at my church and see if anyone can help your family.'

This gave him an idea. He told me that his family had been going to a different church called All Saints in Telford Road. The priest might be able to help, if he knew what had happened to Danu. I promised to ring him. (Mel, the friend who had first introduced me to Danu, would know his number.)

'That is very kind. Thank you,' said Danu.

I saw that he was looking tired. 'I'd better go,' I said. 'You need to rest.'

We said goodbye. When I reached the door, I looked back. He gave me a cheerful wave, but I couldn't help thinking how lonely he looked – a human island in a sea of empty chairs.

I decided I ought to visit him again. I liked him. I liked his courage and unselfishness, and the way he looked at me with those deep, gentle eyes.

In Mazundi there was no love lost between his tribe and mine. If we lived in Mazundi we would never have met. But this was England, and we had met, and I was glad we had. Yes – I would definitely go to see him again.

11

Dark alleys

I was on my way to Charlie's when my mobile rang. It was Kim, who normally only rang when she needed a babysitter. But that wasn't her reason for ringing now.

'I thought I better warn you,' she said. 'Paul O'Farrell's been released.'

'What!' My stomach lurched.

'Yeah. He was back here this afternoon, strolling into the Court like he's the lord of the manor. So it looks like the Old Bill didn't find enough evidence to keep him locked up. If they've got no proof, they can't hold people for more than 24 hours.'

'I don't believe it! How come they didn't find anything at his flat?'

'Well, they were pretty slow off the mark. That mugging was on Wednesday night, wasn't it? And they didn't pick him up until yesterday. If it *was* him that had done it, he had plenty of time to cover up his tracks.'

'It was him all right.' By now, I was feeling extremely scared. If the police hadn't found Paul's knife, did that mean he'd thrown it away? Or had he hidden it in a place where he could find it again? 'But why did you think you ought to warn *me*?'

'Because it was you that grassed him up, wasn't it? You and your brother. I saw you talking to the cops that night, and I thought at the time – that's brave.'

'But we didn't...' Then I stopped protesting. What was the point? It didn't matter if Kim thought we had given Paul's name to the police that night. What Paul thought – that was what mattered.

'All I'm saying is, take care,' said Kim. 'Don't walk down any dark alleys on your own, OK?' And she rang off.

Don't walk down any dark alleys! Oh, terrific. At night, the way into Victory Court was as dark as a deserted coal mine. I decided not to go to Charlie's – safer to go home right away, while it was still daylight.

I could always ring Kwami, but he would be no protection against Paul O'Farrell. Dad was a match for him, but Dad couldn't be there all the time. And if Paul still had his knife, even Dad...

'Shut up! Just shut up,' I said to the fears that came crowding round me like a hostile gang. And then some words from the Bible came into my mind:

I may walk through valleys as dark as death, but I won't be afraid. You are with me...

Mum always said that if you learned verses from the Bible, you were saving up riches in your memory. God would remind you of the words – *his* words – just when you needed them.

Thinking about this, I suddenly realised that a car had pulled up beside me. It was Dad.

'Do you want a lift, or are you trying to ignore me?' he said.

I got in, glad of his company. 'So you got the tyres sorted out,' I said. 'Was it expensive?'

'Yes. I had to get some new ones, and we can't really afford it at the moment. If it happens again... well, it must not happen again. We'll have to park somewhere safer, like near the shops.'

I groaned, because the shops were several minutes' walk away from home. But then I remembered that car tyres were the least of our problems. I told Dad the bad news about Paul.

He went very quiet, and I could see that the news had shaken him. Then he grew angry.

'What use are the police if they can't do anything? The streets are not safe at night. People get stabbed, cars get vandalised, and what do the police do? Nothing! They arrest the guilty ones and then let them go free!'

At least the British police were better than the ones in Mazundi, I thought to myself. The Mazundi police arrested innocent men, and then tortured and killed them. What was happening to the world?

***

John was furious when he heard the news. He started making dark threats about what he would do to Paul O'Farrell, such as spray-painting his motorbike, or even cutting the brake cables.

'John, you are not to do anything like that,' Dad ordered him. 'Stay out of trouble.'

'But it's so unfair! Why should Paul O'Farrell get away with what he did? And his sisters, too. Aren't you going to do anything about the tyres?'

'I told the police about the tyres. But there's no proof that it was the O'Farrells who did it.'

'Told the police? What good will that do?' said Kwami bitterly.

Later, in the kitchen, I found Kwami looking through the drawer where Mum keeps the knives. He jumped guiltily when he heard me come in.

'Kwami! You know what Dad said about carrying knives,' I said, horrified. 'And anyway, most of those are blunt.'

'I wouldn't actually *use* a knife. I just want it for show. You know… if anyone threatens me.'

'I don't think you should,' I said.

'OK, I won't.'

The fact that he agreed so easily, without arguing, made me pretty sure he was planning to ignore what I said.

'Mum will notice if you take any of her knives,' I warned him.

'I told you, I'm not going to! But listen, what am I supposed to do if Paul pulls a knife on me? Stand there and let him slit me from here to here?'

'I just think that if you carry a knife, it's easy for things to… you know… get out of control.'

'They already are,' he said grimly. He pushed past me and went out, slamming the door behind him.

***

We were all very jumpy for the next few days. But nothing happened.

We never parked the car in the same place twice. We made sure the flat was well locked up, front and back, even when we were indoors. When Mum went off to do the night shift, Dad always walked to the car with her. (Coming back in the morning was safer because it was daylight by then.)

John got restless because he couldn't go out. His bruised ribs were starting to feel better, and he wanted to play football when his friends came home from school. But Dad had told him to stay indoors, so he stayed, grumbling all the time. He had to try to be quiet during the day while Mum was sleeping, too, which made him grumble even more.

For the last three days of term I got a lift to school with Charlie's mum, and walked back home with Kwami as my bodyguard. That is, he was *supposed* to be my bodyguard, but he spent most of his time talking to Emma.

'I wish he'd hurry up and ask her out,' Charlie said, as we walked along behind them.

'He's quite shy,' I said. 'He might not look it, but he is.'

'Emma should ask *him* out, then. Strike a blow for feminism.'

'I bet she won't.'

'So it's a stalemate, then. They'll go on walking home together for the next 15 years.'

'Yeah, that's what it looks like.'

'Oh, cheer up, Abena,' Charlie said. 'Are you still worried about that Paul guy? Maybe he's not going to give you grief. Getting arrested might have taught him a lesson.'

Actually, I hadn't been thinking about Paul at all. My mind had been on Danu. For some reason, he often came into my mind.

I had done as he asked and rung his parish priest. I'd also looked after his brother and sister on Sunday afternoon, so that his mother could visit him. This time the kids were happier to stay with me, and his mother was very grateful.

I hadn't gone back to see him, though. I wanted to go, but I also felt afraid. He seemed to have forgotten about our first meeting, at the sleepout, but if we got to know each other better now, he would be bound to find out more about me... where I was born, which tribe I belonged to. Would we end up as enemies, not friends?

In the end I decided it was a risk I had to take. Tomorrow was the last day of school before the Christmas holidays, and lessons finished early. I would go to see him then, and tell him the truth.

12

The den

Danu was in the day room again, but not propped up on pillows any more. He looked much better, I thought, as I crossed the room towards him. He didn't notice my arrival – all his attention was fixed on the TV.

On the screen was a picture of President Baretse. It was the official picture which was everywhere in Mazundi – in shops, on posters, and even in my cousin's school. His face was kindly looking, almost fatherly. He didn't look like a man who would have his opponents tortured to death.

'… and we don't yet know how his death will affect this country, already unstable after three years of civil war,' a reporter was saying. 'Baretse belonged to the Zansi tribe who form two-thirds of Mazundi's population. The minority of Gwema people claim that they have been unfairly treated during his 20-year term as President. His assassination is widely believed to have been carried out by Gwema rebels, in revenge for the massacre at Mbeka.'

'He's been assassinated?' I gasped.

'Yes! They blew up his car,' said Danu, without taking his eyes from the TV. He looked extremely happy. 'Maybe now there is some hope for our country.'

'Or maybe it'll make things worse,' I said. 'More revenge. More killing.'

The TV reporter seemed to agree with me. The camera showed him on the roof of a hotel.

'I don't know if you can hear the gun shots in the background,' he said. 'I've been hearing them on and off all afternoon, ever since the news of Baretse's death became public. Although Baretse was unpopular in the later years of his presidency, his people may still want to take revenge on his supposed killers. I am afraid this country may descend even deeper into the bloodbath of civil war... This is Thomas Okwekwe in Zaro, capital of Mazundi.'

That was the end of the news item. The London studio took over, talking about some other crisis. Danu sighed, and turned to look at me for the first time.

'Abena!' That shining smile again. 'It is nice to see you. I am sorry I did not say hello. I was looking at the news of my country.'

I took a deep breath. 'Actually, it's my country too.'

'Your country?' he said, looking surprised.

'I should have told you before... well, I did tell you, but I don't think you remember... I was born in Mazundi. My family are Zansi.'

Seeing the shock on his face, I said quickly, 'Look, Danu, we don't have to be enemies. This is England, not Mazundi. The war is thousands of miles away.'

'Zansi,' he said. Just the one word, as if he couldn't believe what I'd said.

'Yes, but listen. My family – we didn't like Baretse any more than you did. My father's best friend was killed because he protested against him.'

I stopped, because I could see he wasn't taking in a word I said.

'You are Zansi,' he said slowly. 'But you saved my life.'

'Yes, and I would do it again, anytime. *Love your enemies*, it says in the Bible. And that's another thing. We are both Christians – how can we hate each other?'

He put out his hand, and I took it. 'You are right. We cannot hate each other. In the sight of God we are both his children.'

'Yes, brother.'

'Yes, sister.'

It was a moment of perfect understanding. If only our two tribes could meet like this, I thought – as individual people, not as a mob. The war would be over instantly.

'It is best if you do not tell my mother you are Zansi,' Danu said. 'Not yet.'

'I won't, if you don't tell my family you are Gwema.'

Then we both laughed.

***

I went home feeling very happy. We had talked for ages about all kinds of things. My memories of Mazundi... Danu's first impressions of England... our families... our favourite music... everything. I stayed until late afternoon. Dusk was starting to fall as I came towards Victory Court.

Although there was enough light to see by, I still didn't like going through that archway. I always looked around cautiously in case anyone was lying in wait. Stupid, really. Paul O'Farrell probably wouldn't choose the same place twice... or would he?

Suddenly I froze. There was someone at the far end of the passage, pressed against the wall.

He hadn't seen me. He was facing towards the courtyard, as if he was waiting for the chance to sneak out when no one was looking. But it couldn't be Paul, or even Robbie – they weren't tall enough. It was probably just one of the local kids playing hide-and-seek.

Then, when he heard me, he turned towards me. It was John. The guilty look on his face reminded me that he wasn't supposed to be outside.

'What are you doing? Dad told you to stay indoors,' I said.

'I am indoors.'

'In the flat, I mean. What are you doing?'

He kicked the wall. 'I got so bored. I've been inside for days and days. It's like being in prison. Why should I be the one in prison? I haven't done anything wrong!'

He still hadn't answered my question, so I asked again. 'What are you doing here? Playing solo hide-and-seek – hide, then try to find yourself?'

'Exploring,' he said mysteriously.

'What is there to explore?'

'Robbie's den in the basement. Want to see it?'

He pointed to a doorway at the side of the passage, with a faded sign above it: *Boiler Room. Keep Out.* The lock on the door had been broken years ago. I knew there were steps inside going down to the basement, because I had been in there once, when a friend dared me to. (She told me the basement was haunted by the ghost of the long-dead caretaker, but I never saw him.)

'There's nothing in there except rubbish and rats,' I said.

'That's what you think. Robbie's got a proper den down there. I bet he sleeps there sometimes.'

'Why would he want to sleep down there?' I said. 'Even his pigsty of a flat would be better.'

But by now I was feeling curious. I wanted to take a look, except for one thing – Robbie might catch us in the act.

'You needn't worry,' said John. 'Robbie went out on the motorbike with Paul. I saw them leave, or else I wouldn't have gone in there – I'm not stupid.'

'Yes, but they might come back anytime.'

'With the amount of noise that bike makes, we'll hear them, won't we?' He seemed to have thought it all out.

'OK, then.'

Cautiously I followed him down the steps. He had a torch, but the basement wasn't completely dark. There were small panes of glass overhead, at pavement level, which let in the last of the daylight.

The basement was a big, square room, with four massive boilers. They used to supply hot water to the whole Court, years ago, before each flat got its own central heating. A tangle of pipes, thick with dust, hung on the walls and roof like giant, sleeping snakes. On the floor were heaps of rubbish, broken furniture and a bike with no wheels. There was a smell of dampness and rot.

'Look out for broken needles,' I warned John. 'Like I said – why would Robbie want to sleep here?'

'Oh, this isn't his den. It's over here – look.'

He led me round to the side of one of the huge boilers. I still couldn't see any signs of human life, but then John pointed upwards.

Some planks had been laid across the pipes in the corner, up near the ceiling. They made a platform, a bit like the tree house that Kwami's friends built in the park years ago. It looked as if the only way to get up there was to climb up the pipes – which I had no desire to do.

'I climbed up to have a look,' John said, looking proud of himself. 'He's got a sleeping bag and an old mattress up there.'

'Is that all? No hoard of stolen property?'

'Only some empty beer cans and a couple of magazines. But I bet he would hate to find out I'd been up there.'

There was a sudden scuttering noise in the corner, amongst the rubbish. *Rats!* I absolutely hate rats.

'Come on,' I said to John. 'I'm going.'

He followed me slowly. 'Maybe I could find a dead rat – a nice, rotten one – and put it in his sleeping bag,' he said. 'Like a Christmas present?'

'Probably the only one he'll get. C'mon, get a move on, John! This place is giving me the creeps.'

We came out cautiously, taking care that no one saw us. But we needn't have worried; Paul's parking place was still empty. And at home, Mum was just waking up. She hadn't missed John at all.

I told her the news about President Baretse. Immediately she tried to phone our cousins in Mazundi, but she couldn't get through. Thousands of other people must be trying to ring their cousins, parents, brothers and friends.

'I'll try again later,' she said, looking worried.

John said, 'Aren't you glad that he's dead, Mum? You always said he was an evil man, ruining the country.'

'However bad he was, killing him isn't the answer,' Mum said. 'It could even make things worse. We should all pray for Mazundi.'

13

Near miss

At last, after several tries, Mum managed to get through to our cousins. They were all safe so far. In their hometown things were fairly peaceful, but they'd heard there was fighting in the nearby city. It was hard to get definite news of what was going on. The national TV channel had stopped broadcasting; the radio stations gave conflicting reports.

When he came home, Dad flicked through the TV channels, looking for news.

'... renewed outbreaks of violence in Zaro, the capital of Mazundi, where President Baretse was assassinated this morning. There are rumours of Government troops driving through the north of the city, where many Gwema people live, shooting people at random in revenge for the death of their leader. Meanwhile, the Gwema rebels are said to be making rapid progress towards the capital, destroying Zansi towns and villages which stand in their way.

'Tonight, the future of Mazundi hangs in the balance. The death of the President may be the first of many deaths, as the different factions fight for power, ripping the country to pieces.'

It was frightening. I thought of Miriam, my favourite cousin, who was the same age as me. Instead of looking forward to Christmas, she must be feeling anxious and scared. She was probably packing up as much as she could carry, in case the fighting reached her hometown.

If I had to do that, what would I take with me? I certainly couldn't pack everything into a rucksack. I would have to choose what to take and what to leave behind. And then, if fighting broke out, the whole house – the whole town – might go up in flames!

Oh, God, please keep my cousins safe. Please keep their town peaceful... don't let the people of Mazundi destroy each other...

We went to bed later than usual. I couldn't sleep. I kept thinking about my cousins, and the danger they were in. I had almost forgotten that we ourselves might be in danger. In other places besides Mazundi, there were hearts full of hatred.

***

The next morning, John wanted to do some Christmas shopping. Mum said he could go out, as long as Kwami went with him.

'I can't,' said Kwami. 'I'm working today.' He had a part-time job at a local burger bar.

'I could go,' I said to Mum.

'All right, but make sure you don't stay out too long. I know the O'Farrells seem to have calmed down, but you can't be too careful.' She yawned. It was past her bedtime.

'Anything you want from the shops, Mum?' I asked.

'Oh, I'm glad you reminded me. Mrs Hoskins asked if we could get her some paraffin for her heater. The can's in the hall.'

'Terrific.' Why hadn't I kept my big mouth shut? 'That stuff weighs a ton, Mum.'

But Mum had gone into the bedroom and shut the door.

John and I set off for the shops. I could guess already what he was going to buy – cheap body spray for Mum and me, a T-shirt for Kwami and some socks for Dad. He bought the same kind of thing every year.

I wondered what would be Danu's ideal present, if I was to buy him one. Which of course I wasn't. After all, I hardly knew him – it wasn't as if we were going out together or anything. But if I *did* buy him something… something warm to wear maybe (he still wasn't used to the English weather), or a CD. We'd found that we both liked the same kind of music.

It was quite a successful trip. I bought my last remaining presents. John couldn't manage to find a T-shirt for Kwami, so he bought him, guess what – socks.

'You have no imagination,' I told him. 'Let's get the paraffin, then we can go home.'

We were just five minutes from home when it happened. At a pedestrian crossing, John pressed the button and we waited the usual age for the lights to change. It was on Bridge Street, a busy main road, with traffic whizzing past. At last the lights changed and the cars slowed to a stop. We started to cross, just as a train clattered across the railway bridge.

Because of the train, I never heard the motorbike. I saw it out of the corner of my eye – a sudden glimpse of movement between the two lines of stopped cars. Pure instinct halted me in my tracks. But John hadn't seen it – he was still walking forwards.

'John!' I screamed, and grabbed him by the arm.

The bike roared by, blasting us with noise and a whirlwind of air. A second later it was gone, under the bridge and away.

'That was close,' I said rather shakily. 'Are you all right?'

He nodded. He was staring in the direction the motorbike had taken. The crossing was still beeping out its 'safe to cross' signal, regardless.

John said, 'You know who that was, don't you?'

I didn't answer. I wanted to get safely onto the pavement, and make sure I still had all my shopping – not to mention my fingers and toes.

'It was Paul O'Farrell. He was wearing that jacket with the skull painted on the back.' John's voice was shaky too, but not with fear – with fury. 'And he did it on purpose.'

'No. He wouldn't be that stupid. If he hit us, he could have got knocked off the bike.'

'I bet that didn't even come into his head. He's crazy – you know that. And he hates us. So, he sees his chance. He revs up and comes straight for us.'

'Well, he missed, thank God,' I said.

'Why are we letting him do this?' John cried. 'We can't let him get away with stuff all the time! Someone has to stop him!'

All the way home he went on about it. 'Next time, he could kill somebody. He's a nutter. We ought to stop him!'

'Yeah, I might agree with you, if I could think of a way to do it,' I said wearily. 'Come on, John. I want to get home.'

We couldn't deliver Mrs Hoskins' paraffin because she had gone out to Bingo. I left the can in our hall and started getting lunch for John and me, trying to do it quietly because Mum was sleeping. Halfway through, I heard the noise of a motorbike echoing around the walls of the courtyard. Paul was back.

We watched from the window as Paul chained up his bike in the usual place. Then he went across the court to the staircase. As Kim had said, he strolled around like the lord of the manor.

'Look at him,' said John. 'He's so big-headed. He thinks he can do whatever he likes. I hate him! I hate him!'

I should have said something – I nearly did. But to be honest, at that moment I didn't feel like loving my enemy; I hated him almost as much as John did. It was time someone taught him a lesson.

I went back to getting lunch. A minute later, John came in, saying he needed an empty bottle.

'What for? Have you looked in the recycling box?'

'No, I'll try there.'

When the soup was ready, I went to tell John. Strange – there was a strong, chemical smell as I crossed the hallway. It came from near the door, by the can of paraffin. Looking closer, I saw that there were some splashes on the carpet.

Had John been pouring paraffin from the can into a bottle? Uh-oh! I had a bad feeling about this...

There was the sound of running feet on the balcony, then someone leaning hard on the doorbell.

'Let me in, quick.' It was John's voice – I hurried to open the door. He came in, shut the door hastily, and double-locked it. He was breathing hard, as if he'd run all the way up the stairs. And he seemed to be trying not to laugh.

'What's going on?'

'Nothing.'

But he gave the game away by going to the front window, standing behind the curtain to look out. I followed him. There was a column of dark grey smoke rising up from the courtyard, and at its base, burning brightly, was Paul's motorbike.

'John, did you do that?' I stared at him in disbelief. 'Are you totally mad?'

'It's all right. There was nobody about – I mean, none of the O'Farrells. I checked. It was quite safe.'

'But the whole thing could have exploded! It still could! And look at those kids down there.' Three small children seemed to be daring each other to get up close to the flames, until a woman came out and dragged them away.

A few people watched from the far side of the courtyard. One of them used a mobile, perhaps to call the fire brigade, but no one tried to put out the flames.

That motorbike had woken up too many people at one in the morning.

And no one went to tell Paul. They were probably afraid to.

By the time we heard the fire engine coming, there wasn't much left of Paul's beloved bike. It must have been the siren that alerted Paul to what was going on. He charged out of his flat and down the stairs, yelling and swearing. Two firemen stopped him from going too close to the scene – he aimed a punch at one of them.

Then all the fight seemed to go out of him, as if he realised that nothing could save his motorbike. All that was left was a twisted, blackened pile of scrap metal, and the foul smell of burnt tyres.

John laughed. 'Paul used to boast about burning rubber. I bet he didn't mean this.'

'It isn't funny, John,' I said.

'Yes it is, especially after this morning.'

'That's what I mean. After this morning, he'll know for certain who to blame.'

14

Up in flames

'Hey, have you seen the state of Paul O'Farrell's bike?' said Kwami, as he came in after lunch.

'Yeah,' said John. 'The fire brigade came and everything.'

'He must be really mad. I bet he didn't have any insurance for that thing. He'll have to go out and nick another one,' said Kwami. 'How did the fire start?'

'No idea.'

I never realised my little brother was such a convincing actor. He looked totally innocent.

'Don't tell anyone. Specially not Mum or Dad,' he had begged me earlier, when he began to realise that he might have done something pretty stupid. And I had agreed to keep quiet, although I felt uneasy about the whole thing.

It was probably better that Mum and Dad didn't know. If Dad found out what John had done, he would be furious. He might do something completely crazy, like make John apologise to Paul and offer to pay for the damage. And that wouldn't help matters. It would just make Paul even surer that people were afraid of him.

Anyway, how much would it cost to buy a new motorbike? Hundreds, probably thousands of pounds. We didn't have that kind of money to throw around – especially after buying a new set of car tyres.

So I said nothing. I told myself that my parents already had enough to worry about.

Emma rang me later. She had spent the afternoon helping out at the drop-in centre for homeless people.

'How did it go?' I asked her.

'OK. There were seven people there. Better than last Saturday when they only had three. I suppose it will take time before people get to hear about it.'

'Maybe I could help on Saturday,' I said. 'What do you actually have to do?'

She told me how she had helped with the cooking, and then sorted through several bags of second-hand clothes. 'Honestly, the things people donated! Even if I was homeless and skint, I wouldn't be seen dead in some of them. You know... jumpers full of holes, old shirts covered in paint, and shiny sequinned tops. It's like – oh, these people are homeless, they'll be grateful to get anything.'

Then she lowered her voice. 'Listen, don't tell Charlie this. I don't want to get her hopes up. But I saw a guy who looked a lot like Zack.'

'Zack?' For a minute I couldn't remember who she meant.

'Her brother or half-brother. He's been missing for ages, remember? But I'm not sure if it was actually him.'

'Didn't you ask his name?'

'No, because he only arrived at closing time. That was the worst bit of the whole day – turning everyone out on to the street.'

'If Zack is really in Birton,' I said, 'why doesn't he go to Charlie's house?'

'He must be afraid to go back. You know he stole all that money off Charlie's mum. He probably thinks she would shut the door in his face. But actually she wants him to come back.'

'Yes, and he must want to, or else he wouldn't be here.'

Emma said, 'I wish I'd said something, but I wasn't sure it was him. And it's too late now.'

'Maybe he'll come back,' I said. 'You never know.'

***

Beep... beep... beep...

The noise of the smoke alarm disrupted my dreams, like a rough hand on my shoulder, shaking me awake. The alarm must be playing up again, I thought sleepily. Dad ought to fix it.

Beep... beep... beep... beep...

What was that smell? I sat up in bed and put the light on.

Smoke – that's what the smell was. A thin wisp of smoke was coming in under my door. The flat was on fire!

Still confused with sleep, I got up and opened my bedroom door. Heat hit me in the face, like the opening of an oven. A river of flame was flowing from the front door along the hallway.

'Dad!' I screamed at the top of my voice.

Dad opened his door on the opposite side of the
hall. I wanted to run to him, but that river of fire was
in the way.

'Abena!' he shouted. "You'll have to go out the
back way. Out through the fire door! In the kitchen!'

For a moment, I stood frozen with horror. But this
wasn't a dream; I couldn't dive back under the duvet
and go to sleep again. It was really happening. The
flames were really singeing my feet.

Oh, God! Help me…

I grabbed my nearest shoes and shoved them on.
There wasn't time to pick up anything else. Keeping
close to the wall, I edged my way towards the kitchen
door.

Through the flickering curtain of heat, I saw
Kwami come out of his and John's bedroom, pushing
John ahead of him like a sleepwalker. They would
have to get out through Mum and Dad's window at
the front, onto the balcony.

I opened the kitchen door – and stared in disbelief.
There was fire in here, too. Flames leapt up in front of
the fire exit door, blocking it completely. I could see
the fire extinguisher beside the cooker, but I couldn't
reach it.

Now what?

My bedroom window. It was the only hope – I
could climb out onto the fire escape.

I darted back into my room and shut the door.
Already, my room was filling with smoke. No flames
yet, though. The window was locked, of course. Key
on the sill somewhere – find it. No need to panic.

I found the key. The window opened all right. But on the outside was a metal grille to stop burglars. Different key – where was it?

Above the crackle of flames, the alarm was still beeping loudly. The open window sucked air out of the room and drew smoke in. I coughed until it hurt.

I could not find the key for the security bars. There was too much stuff on the sill. Books, alarm clock, stupid little souvenirs from school trips – I swept them all onto the floor. No key.

'Help!' I screamed into the darkness. There was no answer. I heard a loud *whump* from somewhere in the flat – an explosion? I began to cough again and couldn't stop.

Even though I walk through the valley of the shadow of death,

I will fear no evil, for you are with me...

No shadows in this valley, only the bright river of flame. But death was here all right. I would choke to death from the smoke behind the bars that were meant to protect me.

I will fear no evil, for you are with me. I held onto the thought, and beneath all my panic, I knew God was there, solid as a rock. Rocks don't burn... do they?

Suddenly my mobile rang. I snatched it up from beside my bed.

'Abena, where are you?' It was Dad.

'I'm trapped!' I gasped, choking on my words. 'The kitchen's on fire. And I can't get out of my window!'

'Hold on. I'm coming,' he said. 'And there's a fire engine on its way. Just keep calm. I'm coming right now.'

Dad must have got out at the front of the flat. My window was at the back. He would have to run down the stairs, out of the Court and around the side of the building, and then climb up the fire escape.

And now my door was starting to burn through. The smoke was thick, dark and choking. I got as close to the grille as I could, trying to breathe fresh air.

Far away, I thought I heard a fire engine. Oh, hurry, hurry…

I heard a shout from down below. 'Abena!'

Because of the bars, I couldn't lean out, but I shouted back. I heard the clang of steel, the rattle of a ladder, then feet running along the balcony.

And then Dad's face was there, beyond the bars. 'Pass me the key,' he said.

'I… can't… find it!' Every word was a struggle. 'Help me, Dad…'

'Kwami! I need some tools! A hammer and chisel,' he shouted down. Then he turned back to me. 'Don't be afraid. We'll soon get you out of here.'

Where was Kwami going to find a hammer and chisel at two in the morning? Dad didn't wait to find out. He was trying to get his fingers between the wall and the metal grille. Somehow, by sheer desperate strength, he bent it slightly – just an inch or two, enough to let me touch his hand.

Other people were down there now – I could hear their voices. And the fire engine sounded nearer. But the smoke was so thick, I couldn't see across the room.

You are with me... you are with me... even in the valley of the shadow...

Then Dad let go of my hand. I couldn't help it – I screamed.

His voice was calm, reassuring. 'It's all right. Kwami has brought some tools. Stand back a little, Abena.'

He began hammering away, trying to loosen the fixings of the metal grid. The chisel slipped, slicing at his hand, but he carried on grimly. I saw that Kwami was there too, trying to bend the metal back on itself to make a gap.

They managed to free one side of it at last. Dad pulled it away from the wall.

'Come on, Abena! Climb through!'

I got onto the sill. I squeezed myself sideways through the gap. For a dreadful minute, I thought I'd got stuck. Then, with a last heave, I was through.

Free! I was free! I tried to breathe in the cool, night air. But it felt as if my lungs were blocked with cotton wool. I gasped, and choked, and coughed again.

Dad caught me and held me tight. It was good he did, because I could feel myself swaying, almost fainting.

'I can't climb down that ladder,' I said hoarsely.

'Then I'll carry you.'

'You won't have to. The fire engine's here,' said Kwami.

Looking back, I don't remember much more after that – a confusion of flashing lights and shouting, and the rescue platform swooping up towards us like a lift. And I couldn't stop coughing. I remember that.

There was an ambulance. We all got in. And I remember how John said, quite calmly, 'Everything's gone up in flames, hasn't it? Even my Christmas presents.'

And then I began to realise what I'd lost. Everything I owned… my TV, my CDs, my mobile… my half-finished English coursework… all my clothes… everything.

Oh, God! Why did you let this happen? You could have stopped it! It's so unfair!

'At least we are all alive,' said Dad. 'Thank God for that.'

15

Night shift

The ambulance took us to Birton Royal, the hospital where Mum worked. She told us later that it was the worst moment of her entire life. Three of her family getting out of an ambulance – that was bad enough. But then she saw me on a trolley wearing an oxygen mask.

I had breathed in a lot of smoke. My lungs still felt strange the following day, and I was kept in hospital, breathing oxygen through a tube in my nose. The others were allowed to go home. Except that there was no home to go to.

'The Council has put us in emergency housing,' Dad told me that evening, when he brought John to visit me. 'Two rooms; it's not very nice—'

'It's disgusting,' said John. 'It stinks. You're better off in here, Abena.'

'You think so? I'd swap with you if they let me.'

'And it's Christmas in three days,' John said moodily. 'It should be a great Christmas this year. Not.'

For the twentieth time, I thought of all my carefully chosen presents, most likely ruined by smoke or soaked by the fire-fighters' hoses. And my phone – I was really missing my phone. And what about my clothes? All I had to wear was one pair of shoes, and my pyjamas.

Dad and John were wearing a strange assortment of clothes I had never seen before. Dad's jacket looked too small and John's was too big. John was wearing the sort of ultra-cheap trainers he normally hated.

'The vicar brought round some bags of clothes,' Dad said. 'It was very kind of him.' I could guess where most of the things had come from – the collection for the homeless people. But then, we were pretty close to being homeless ourselves.

I asked Dad how much of my stuff had survived the fire. He said he didn't know, because he hadn't been allowed back into the flat. When he went round there, the police were looking into the cause of the fire – or rather, the two separate causes.

It looked as if the fire had been started deliberately in two different places. Petrol had been poured in through the letterbox at the front. At the back, someone had smashed a pane of glass in the fire door, and poured more petrol on the floor. To ignite it, he – or they, for there must have been two of them – only needed to throw in lighted matches.

'Two people,' I said. 'Paul and Robbie. One at the front, one at the back... I bet Robbie thought of that. It's exactly what he did at Kim's place.'

'They really didn't want us to get out alive,' said John. Suddenly he looked frightened.

I said, 'I heard a sort of explosion, too. What would that have been?'

'The paraffin,' said John. 'There was a whole can of it sitting in the hall. It would explode if it got hot enough, wouldn't it?'

Not quite a whole can, I thought, remembering the motorbike. But it was probably enough to do damage, if it exploded everywhere. I tried to imagine what the flat must look like now – a smoke-blackened ruin, like a scene from a war zone. And the war wasn't over yet.

'Dad, will we have to go back to that flat?' I asked. 'Can't we go and live somewhere else? I mean, somewhere outside Victory Court – a long way away from the O'Farrells.'

'But Paul and Robbie will get done for this,' said John. 'They will, won't they, Dad?'

'I don't know. That depends on what the police managed to find.' He didn't seem confident. 'If there are no fingerprints, and no one saw who did it, the police won't be able to prove it was them.'

My heart sank like a stone. If the O'Farrells got away with it, I wouldn't be able to sleep peacefully in that flat, ever again.

Dad said, 'I am going to ask the Council to rehouse us, but I don't know if they will agree. It's not only us, you know. The fire affected the neighbours on both sides, and on the floor above. They can't suddenly find new homes for all of us.'

He sounded defeated. I hated seeing Dad – so strong, so brave against physical danger – looking so helpless. He didn't believe in violence; he believed in the law. But the law had already let us down once.

The only other option was to move away. And we couldn't even do that, if the Council would not rehouse us. If we did, we would be homeless – even more homeless than we were already.

'Where is this temporary flat?' I asked.

John said, 'It's not a flat – it's two rooms, that's all, and no telly or anything.'

'In Hill Street,' said Dad.

'You don't mean Gordon House?'

'It's called Andrews House.'

John said, 'It's just up the road from where your friends live. The ones I got the toys for.' He thought about this. 'That's weird. That's the only stuff that didn't get ruined – the stuff we gave away.'

***

In the middle of the night, I woke up to find a nurse asleep in the chair by my bedside. Then I realised that it was Mum. She'd gone to work as usual because they were short-staffed in Casualty. She was on her break in the middle of the night shift.

'I wasn't going to wake you,' she whispered. 'I just wanted to make sure you were all right.'

'You were asleep, Mum. Don't deny it.'

'I was praying,' she said.

'Praying for me? Don't worry, I feel a lot better. Honest.'

'For all of us. For the whole situation.'

My small side ward, with just two other beds in it, was calm and quiet. The only sound was the hum of hospital equipment, and the gentle snoring of the girl opposite. It was almost as peaceful as an empty church.

But I didn't feel peaceful inside. Whenever I thought about what had happened to us, I felt angry and resentful. I had lost that feeling of closeness to God. I couldn't even pray.

'Mum… why do you think God let this happen?'

For a minute she said nothing. Then she said, 'I don't know. God doesn't always stop bad things from happening. He never promised us an easy life, but he did promise always to be with us through everything that happens.'

Yes… in the fire, I had known the truth of that. But I didn't know it any more. I felt as if God was far away, invisible, like the sun hidden behind heavy clouds.

Mum said, 'God always lets people choose what to do. If they choose evil, he doesn't interfere with that choice. But he sees and he knows. And after they die there will be a judgement.'

'And the bad people will be punished?'

She nodded. 'But you see, we are all bad. None of us makes the right choice every time. We all choose evil sometimes. Jesus said that being angry with people was evil, as evil as killing them. I don't know about you, but I am often angry, even though I know it's wrong…'

'Yes,' I whispered, 'I get angry, too.'

'And I've made other wrong choices – hundreds of them. But I have asked God to forgive me for them. And whenever we do that, the page is wiped clean – completely clean. All the bad things are forgiven.'

I knew all this – of course, I did. But the next thing she said took me by surprise.

'There is something that stops us from being forgiven, though. Do you know what it is?'

I shook my head.

'If we don't forgive other people, then God won't forgive us. That's what Jesus said.' She put out her hand and took mine. 'So I am trying to forgive the O'Farrells for what they did to us. I am trying not to hate them and feel angry with them. It isn't easy!'

'That's an understatement,' I muttered.

Mum looked at her watch, and got up hurriedly. 'I must get back. I'll come and see you again when I go off duty.'

She leaned over and kissed me. Then she hurried off down the corridor.

The things she'd said went round and round in my head. *If we don't forgive other people, then God won't forgive us.*

But I didn't want to forgive my enemies. What they had done was too terrible. I couldn't just turn round and say, 'Oh, it doesn't matter what you did to us. I really don't care about it. Have a nice day!'

Somewhere down the corridor, a medical alarm went off – beeping like our smoke alarm – and feet went hurrying by. A trolley went past, its wheels squeaking. The girl in the bed opposite gave a restless moan.

It took me ages to get back to sleep.

16

Grim and depressing

By the next morning my breathing was much better, and in the afternoon the doctor said I could leave the hospital. She gave me an inhaler to use if I had problems, and told me to come back at once if I started feeling bad again.

Dad came to pick me up. He'd brought some clothes which Emma had lent me. They looked better than the things people had donated – in fact, the pink top was one of her favourites. 'And Emma says that if you would like to, you can go and stay with her until we get sorted out,' Dad said.

I wasn't sure about this. What I really wanted was to be with my family, somewhere safe and secure, a long way from the O'Farrells. If only we could all have gone to Emma's house! But they didn't have enough room.

Dad could see that I was in two minds. 'Come back to Andrews House,' he said. 'You can see what it's like, and then decide.'

Andrews House was quite close to where Danu lived. It was a similar big, old-fashioned house which had been split up into sections. And it was similarly grim and depressing inside. We had been allocated two rooms, but Mum would need to sleep in one

during the daytime. That left just one room for all the
rest of us to sit in, cook in, eat in, watch TV (if we had
one), quarrel, fight and go mad in.

As if that wasn't bad enough, it was only a few
minutes away from Victory Court. I could see the top
floor flats above the rooftops.

'They said this was the only place they had,' said
Dad. 'It's only temporary.'

Kwami said, 'Temporary? Yeah, right. That's what
they told Danu about his place. And he's been there
for weeks and weeks.'

'Who's Danu?' Dad asked him.

'He's the guy that got stabbed. I bumped into him
today – he only lives down the road. I recognised him
straight away.'

'So he's out of hospital! Is he all right?' I asked. *Did
he ask about me?* was what I really wanted to say. But
then, Kwami didn't know I had been visiting Danu.

Of course, Danu was one reason for choosing to
stay here, and my family was another. But I could see
that life would be a lot easier if I went to Emma's –
easier for everyone else, too. There would be more
space, and my parents would have one less person to
worry about.

So I decided to go to Emma's, at least for a few
days.

'But what about Christmas?' said John. 'We have to
be together for Christmas!' He sounded almost
panicky, as if he felt our family was falling apart.

'Of course we will,' said Dad. We'd had several
invitations from friends at church, as soon as people

heard what had happened to us. We were going to the Jackson's for Christmas dinner and the Karendes' for Boxing Day. Which was just as well, because we didn't have as much as one piece of tinsel to decorate our new home, or one chicken leg to eat.

'Can I get some things from the flat?' I asked Dad.

'Not yet. We're not supposed to touch anything until the insurance assessor has looked at the place.'

'Can't I even see if my phone is still usable?'

He shook his head. 'It's all locked up.'

So it was easy for me to pack my things. I had nothing at all except the clothes I was wearing, and even those weren't really mine.

The next day was Sunday – Christmas Eve. I went to the morning service with Emma. (You can't really skip church when you are living in a vicarage.) But I wasn't at all in the mood for Christmas.

I watched the Sunday Club kids doing the usual Nativity Play. I sang the usual carols. None of it seemed to mean anything – it was like a children's story that I'd heard too many times. Looking around the church, with its candles and holly and Christmas flowers, I thought of the cold, grey rooms where my family had to live.

What kind of Christmas would the O'Farrell family have? A terrible one, I was secretly hoping. Their mum would have spent all her money on booze. She would be too drunk to buy presents or cook a meal. Her sons would quarrel and fight – the knife would come out – Paul would end up in the police cells, and Robbie in Casualty. Oh yes, and the twins would try to cook something, get food poisoning and be as sick as dogs...

I knew I shouldn't be thinking like this. Especially when Emma whispered, 'What's the matter? You look angry.'

I tried to smooth my face out into an expression more suitable for a church service. *Love your enemies, do good to those who hate you.* But it was hard, so hard to do that. How could I keep on doing it, when it didn't make any difference? When I'd lost my home and everything I owned? When the enemy always seemed to win? When things just got worse and worse?

***

After lunch, Emma helped me by digging out a few things to give my family for Christmas. A box of sweets, a book donated by Emma's mum, a CD of Emma's... oh yes, and some socks. We wrapped them all up, so at least there would be something for people to unwrap. I wished I had something to give Emma, but I couldn't exactly make her a present of her own CD. And I had absolutely no money.

The TV news was on. I wasn't really watching it until they started talking about the trouble in Mazundi. More fighting between Zansi and Gwema... more refugees streaming out of the city... it looked as if those people would be having an even worse Christmas than mine.

The announcer said, 'Today, Mazundi national TV broadcast an appeal for peace and reconciliation.'

The screen showed the face of a man of around Dad's age. He was speaking Gwema, but an English voice-over had been added.

'I am calling for an end to the hatred,' he said. 'That is a hard thing to ask. It's much easier to hate than to love. We can warm ourselves with the flame of our hatred. It glows and burns inside us, and feeds on thoughts of revenge.

'But fire is dangerous. When it gets out of control, it can destroy a whole forest, an entire country. There is nothing left then, only scorched and twisted branches.'

I stared at the TV. *Daniel Obindi, writer,* was the caption at the foot of the screen.

Could this be Danu's father? His voice reminded me of Danu, and so did his face – except that he wasn't smiling. As for the name, I was almost sure Danu's last name was Obindi.

He went on, 'For the sake of our land, for the lives of our children, we must try to forgive each other for the wrongs of the past. Forgiveness is more than just words. It means taking action. It means treating my enemy as if he is my brother. If we cannot do this, our country will destroy itself.'

I wanted to tell Danu about this. He would be very happy to know that his father was safe and well – if it *was* his father.

If only I could have rung Danu! But he didn't have a mobile, or a TV either, come to that. And now the man's face was no longer on screen. He had been replaced by someone talking about football scores.

Just then, Charlie rang. She was planning to go out and invite homeless people to the Christmas meal at St Judes, and she wanted us to go with her. Emma and I agreed to go. I could always call in on Danu on the way back.

It wasn't as cold as the last time we went out. A thin drizzle of rain blew against our faces. Down by the railway arches there was no sign of the old men. The bag lady was there though, with her shopping trolley. She promised to come to the Christmas meal.

'Oh yes, I'll be there, dear. Unless I get a better offer, that is!' She cackled with laughter.

'And bring anyone else you know who'd like to come,' said Emma.

'You should ask that young man,' she said, pointing towards the farthest arch. 'He's new around here, and if you ask me, he's in a bad way. No flesh on his bones at all. Needs fattening up!'

In the shelter of the arch, with an old sleeping bag wrapped around him, a boy sat staring at the ground. As soon as she saw him, Charlie's steps quickened.

'Zack!' she called out, and he turned to look. 'Zack! Is it really you?'

A slow smile crept onto his face, and I saw that it was her brother all right. But he looked different from the last time I'd seen him. He looked quite ill, actually. His face was as grey as old newspapers, and he was shivering.

'Why didn't you come home?' said Charlie. 'We've been waiting for you.'

'I wanted to come,' he said. His voice was hoarse and rough. 'But I didn't know if you would want me.'

'Because of the money, you mean? Don't worry about that. Mum forgave you for that ages ago. Come home, Zack! It'll be the best Christmas present Mum could have.'

'Are you sure?' he asked, looking as if he couldn't believe her.

'Yes! I'll ring her right now.'

She talked excitedly to her mum. Then she said to Zack, 'She's coming to pick us up in the car. She'll be here in five minutes. See? I told you it would be all right.'

But Zack still looked worried until Charlie's mum arrived. She jumped out of the car and came hurrying over. Her smile was brighter than the star on a Christmas tree.

Now, I could see, he believed what Charlie had told him. He struggled to his feet, the effort making him cough painfully.

'I'm really sorry,' he said to Charlie's mum. 'When I get some money, I'll—'

'Never mind that – I'm just glad you're here. We missed you so much, Zack!' And she gathered him up in a hug.

Emma and I watched them drive away. I was pleased for them, but all the same I couldn't help thinking that Zack might not be there for very long. His problem had been an obsession with gambling. I wondered if he'd changed.

'If I was Charlie's mum,' said Emma, 'I wouldn't leave any money lying around the house. Come on; let's find a few more people before it gets dark.'

17
Evacuate!

On the way back, I persuaded Emma we should go by way of Hill Street. But when I rang Danu's doorbell, there was no answer.

Oh, well... why not call in and see my family? It was less than 24 hours since I'd seen them, but already I was missing them.

It was John who answered the door. He told me Mum and Dad had gone out to try and get some Christmas things. 'But your friend's here,' he said.

'My friend?'

'That boy, Danu. He belongs to the Gwema tribe – did you know?'

'That doesn't mean he's our enemy,' I said. 'But why is he here?'

'Kwami met him yesterday. He came around today and they've been talking for ages. Kwami told me to go away,' John said resentfully. 'I mean, where is there to go?'

We all went up to the rooms. I could see Emma was quite shocked by the place, although she didn't say anything. It was all so grimy and grubby from the dozens of people who had passed through it. The furniture was ancient; the beds sagged, the wardrobe wouldn't stay shut and was depressingly empty. There was only one sign of Christmas – a lone card on the mantelpiece.

John knocked on the connecting door to the other room. 'Abena's here,' he called. 'And Emma.'

Danu looked pleased to see me. Kwami smiled at Emma. All the same, there was an atmosphere in the room, as if we had interrupted something – serious talking, or some kind of secret plan. What was going on?

I told Danu about the TV programme I'd seen. At the name 'Daniel Obindi', his face lit up.

'You are right. It was my father. What did he say?'

'He said that people have to stop hating each other. Hatred can burn you up, he said. If people go on fighting and can't forgive what happened in the past, they'll destroy each other.' I wished I could remember his exact words.

'Forgive!' Kwami said angrily. 'What's the good of forgiving people? They'll just keep on doing what they do! They'll never change!'

I said, 'But Danu's father was right. If people don't change their ways, Mazundi will—'

'I'm not talking about Mazundi,' Kwami interrupted. 'I'm talking about the O'Farrells. Look what they did to us. They almost killed you and Danu, and they ruined our flat – and so far they've got away with it. But not any more!'

'What do you mean?'

'I mean we're going to teach them a lesson. If the police won't do it, we'll have to find some other way of paying them back. Isn't that right, Danu?'

Danu looked awkward. I wondered if he was thinking about what his father had said – because I certainly was. What was true for Mazundi was true here, too.

'No!' I cried. 'Can't you see how useless it is? You get back at them – then they get back at us – it never ends. It won't stop until somebody gets killed! Maybe not even then!'

Kwami said, 'You've forgotten something, Abena. We know where they live, but they don't know where to find us. So that puts us ahead of them.'

'What are you going to do?' asked John.

'Smash their windows, for a start.'

'Good idea,' said John. 'Can I come too?'

Kwami said, 'No. It's too dangerous. Stay here, John, ready to let us back in. We might have to move fast.'

Danu was still looking unsure what to do. I said urgently, 'Danu, what would your father think of this? He said we have to try to make peace, not get revenge.'

'Don't listen to her,' Kwami said. 'She's just a girl. She gets scared.'

Danu looked from Kwami to me, then back at Kwami. *Oh God... please help him to choose the right thing! Please don't let Kwami persuade him!*

'Come on,' Kwami said impatiently.

'No. I have decided,' said Danu. 'Abena is right. I should listen to the words of my father.'

Kwami gave him a scornful look. 'And I should have listened to the words of my grandfather. Never trust a scorpion, a snake or a Gwema.'

Without another word to any of us, he went out, slamming the door. I ran to the window. There was another slam of a door, and I saw him heading up the road in the direction of Victory Court.

I wished Dad and Mum would come back. When Kwami got in a mood like this, he wouldn't pay attention to anyone except Dad. But John had no idea when they would be home. And I couldn't ring Mum because I didn't know her mobile number. It was on my own mobile, probably destroyed in the fire.

'I should go after Kwami,' I said. I had a feeling of dread in my stomach. Something bad – something *else* bad – was about to happen.

Emma said, 'I'll come too,' and Danu picked up his jacket.

'Stay here,' I told John. 'As soon as Dad gets back, tell him what's happening.'

We went out into the rain and the darkness.

But there was no sign of Kwami at Victory Court. And the O'Farrells' flat looked deserted, the windows unlit. The wrecked motorbike had been cleared away, leaving a dark brown stain on the concrete.

I wanted to take a look at our flat, or what was left of it. So we went upstairs. The front door was padlocked, and the outside wall was blackened with smoke above the boarded-up windows. The flats on either side and above us also had their doors secured shut and windows boarded up. The whole place had a horrible, empty feeling.

Then a door opened behind us, and Mrs Hoskins peered out. She looked worried.

'Abena! Is that you? You won't get in, you know, it's all locked up. But come here a mo. Tell me – can you smell gas?'

I stepped inside her door. The usual smell in her hallway was an overpowering odour from her paraffin heater. (The gas central heating was too expensive, she said.) But I thought I could smell something else as well. After a couple more sniffs, I was sure of it.

'You've got a gas leak,' I told her.

'But my gas is turned off,' she said, puzzled. 'How can it be leaking?'

'I don't know, but I think you should call the gas people.'

'Oh dear, I never did like gas,' she said. 'I don't trust it. In the war we had some terrible gas explosions, worse than the bombs sometimes.'

Because she was so nervous, I stayed with her while she rang the gas company.

'They're sending someone round at once,' she said. 'And I have to open all my windows, and not use anything electrical. Oh dear, and it's Christmas Eve! I hope they get it sorted out before tomorrow.'

Danu went further along the balcony, past our flat. Then he went upstairs to the level above. Coming back, he said, 'That smell is there, too. It is very strong.'

'It must be a bad leak,' said Emma. 'Could it be something to do with the fire? Maybe a pipe got damaged, or something.'

'This is an old building,' I said. 'The pipes must be pretty old, too.'

Mrs Hoskins said, 'I expect we'll have to evacuate the whole place – just like in the war!' She sounded quite excited. 'Look, dear, don't wait around here. It might be dangerous. You'll be safer out in the street. Go on, now.'

'Are you sure you'll be all right?'

'I'll be fine. Look, here comes the gas man now.' A yellow van marked *Central Gas Company* had just arrived. 'Yoo-hoo! Up here, young man!'

I remembered we were looking for Kwami. There was still no sign of him in Victory Court. Perhaps he'd gone back to Andrews House, and we had missed him.

We went out into the street. But before we had gone very far, another yellow van arrived at top speed, lights flashing. It was closely followed by a fire engine, and I could hear all the alarms going off inside Victory Court. Mrs Hoskins was right. They were going to evacuate the building.

A thin trickle of people began coming out of the archway. Soon it swelled into a crowd, complete with children, pets, and favourite possessions hurriedly snatched up. (I saw Dexter carrying a hamster cage, which didn't do much for his street cred.) A policeman directed everyone down Hill Street, towards the community centre.

We watched them go. Meanwhile, the police were setting up traffic cones across the road, and diverting traffic away from Victory Court.

'Wow! They're taking this seriously,' said Emma.

And so was I – because there was still no sign of Kwami.

Then I saw the O'Farrell twins coming up the road from the shops. They had probably been doing some shoplifting for their mum. They asked a policeman what was going on, and he explained.

'Go down to the community centre,' he told them. 'I expect your mum's there already, and if not, she soon will be.'

'But we want to go up to the flat. I bet she's still there.'

'Yeah, she never goes out much, see.'

'She just lies on the sofa; sleeps all the time.'

'Specially when she's... had a few.'

The policeman sighed. 'All right, I'll get someone to check your flat again. What number is it?'

'29. And tell them to knock loud.'

'Yeah, the bell's broken.'

At least I knew now where some of the O'Farrells were. But what about Paul and Robbie? Like Kwami, they seemed to have vanished off the face of the earth.

18
Upwards

Among the people leaving the building were Kim and her two daughters. Tara, like Kim, looked as if she was enjoying the excitement. But Kerry, clutching a huge teddy bear, looked rather worried by it all.

'Abena!' cried Kim. 'I thought you'd moved out. What are you doing here?'

'You're right, we have moved,' I said. 'But it's only temporary. They say we have to go back once the flat's been sorted out; which I'm really looking forward to… not.'

'Don't look so fed up. I got some good news for you – Paul O'Farrell's been arrested again.' She lowered her voice. 'And it's all down to me.'

'How?'

'Because I saw him that night – the night of the fire. I don't sleep too good sometimes. That night I'm lying awake, and I hear feet going past my door and stopping outside my window… But hold on. Come over here, out of the rain.'

We sheltered in a pub doorway, which smelt of stale beer. Tara held her nose. The crowd of people streamed endlessly past without seeing us.

Kim went on, 'So I get my phone ready to call 999, and I look out through the blinds. And it's Paul O'Farrell on the balcony. He's standing right up close to my window, like he wants to hide in the shadows. That skull on his jacket is staring me right in the face.

But he doesn't see me – he's watching something on the far side of the courtyard. And I notice he's carrying a petrol can, which is strange, because he doesn't have a motorbike any more.

'And then he moves on, making for his flat, and I see what he's been looking at – your flat's on fire. Someone's climbing out of the front window. So I call the fire brigade, pretty sharpish.'

'Kim!' I cried. I wanted to hug her. 'You probably helped to save my life. But how did the police get to hear about Paul?'

'Shhh. I don't want the O'Farrell brats to hear. I've still got to live on the same landing as them and Robbie.'

'So you didn't see Robbie that night?' I said.

'No, only Paul. But I thought: right, this has got to stop. The guy's a psycho. It might be my place that gets set alight next. So the next day, I went to the police.'

'That was very brave,' I said. 'We never told the police – we rang that anonymous help line.'

'Yeah. Trouble is, if it's anonymous, they can't use it in court. What they need is a statement from somebody who'll stand up in court and say what they saw. And I said to the police, "Look, if I do this, you've got to protect me and my girls. Like, get us moved somewhere else, before the court case comes up." And they said they'll do it.'

'Are you sure the O'Farrells don't suspect it was you that grassed him up?'

'Pretty sure, because Jackie's still speaking to me. She tried to borrow money off me this morning. Said she's got no money for the meter, and can I lend her some 'til she gets her benefits? I told her I'm skint. Seems like the O'Farrells will have a cold, dark Christmas – tragic, eh?'

I smiled to myself. If Paul was safely out of the way, Robbie wouldn't be much of a threat to Kwami. As for the twins... but where were the twins?

They were still outside Victory Court, arguing with the policeman.

'Look, someone's checked your flat,' he was saying. 'All the lights were off, and no one answered the door.'

'Course the lights were off.'

'Cos we ain't got no money for the 'lectric.'

'She's in there all right.'

'We'll go and have a look.'

'No you won't – it's too dangerous,' the policeman said. 'Wait a minute, and I'll get someone to take you down to the community centre.'

The twins looked at each other.

'We know where that is.'

'We can get there on our own, we ain't stupid.'

They joined the last of the stragglers going down Hill Street. A minute later, they somehow seemed to disappear. They had probably climbed over the wall into the car park – because nobody tells the O'Farrells what to do.

Now there was no one coming out of Victory Court. With hardly any windows lit, it looked dark and forbidding, like a castle ready for a siege. The policeman was still on sentry duty by the entrance. Nothing seemed to be happening – at least, nothing that could be seen from here.

'Where could Kwami have got to?' asked Emma. 'There's another way out of the building, isn't there?'

'Yes, at the opposite side,' I said. 'In Canal Street. But I don't see why he would go out that way... unless he was following Robbie.'

'We could go and see,' said Danu.

That would mean a long walk round, if we weren't allowed to go through the Court. And it was still raining. But I knew we couldn't just go home... at least, not yet.

Of course, we could always copy the twins and take a short cut through the car park. Better make sure the policeman doesn't see us, though.

An ambulance came slowly along Hill Street. No flashing lights, no siren – perhaps it was only there as a precaution, in case something happened. The policeman began to move the traffic cones so that it could park opposite the entrance.

'All right, let's go,' I said, 'while he isn't looking.'

The wall was only chest high. It was easy to scramble over it and drop down into the car park. No one shouted after us, no one tried to stop us.

'Car park' was too grand a name for what was really just a bit of waste ground between Victory Court and the wall of an old factory. It was rough underfoot, and badly lit.

A cat ran out from behind some bins, making me jump. There were rain-puddles here and there which were hard to see in the dark. A stone twisted beneath my foot, and I almost fell. I was grateful when Danu took my hand.

And then, from high above us, I heard a thin, piercing scream.

We all stopped instantly.

The scream came again, and a desperate voice cried out, 'Tiffany! Hold on!'

'It's the O'Farrell twins,' I said. 'Little idiots! They must be trying to go up the fire escape.'

The wall of the Court rose up to our right. Light from a street lamp gleamed on the metal fire escape, and the ladders that connected its different levels. High up at the third floor level were two small figures. One was dangling from the balcony, her hands gripping on and her legs swinging about in space.

Danu didn't hesitate. 'Quickly, get help!' he said to us. He shouted up, 'Hold on! I'm coming!'

Emma ran towards the front of the building. But it didn't need two people to do that. And I didn't want to leave Danu on his own.

He was trying to find a way up to the first floor balcony. There was a ladder which could be lowered, but it was in the 'up' position. How had the twins managed to start their climb?

'Danu! Over here! There's a rope ladder,' I shouted.

It looked like something Robbie might have fixed up – an old, fraying rope ladder dangling down from the first level. Danu was up there in a few seconds. I followed more slowly.

Another ladder: a metal one this time, the rungs cold and slippery with rain. I wondered why I was doing this. Why bother? Why should I care what happened to the O'Farrell twins? They wouldn't care about me... I suddenly realised that I was doing it for Danu's sake.

He was well ahead of me. Before I got off the ladder, he'd already reached the screaming girl, who hung from the outside of the balcony above. He grabbed her by the knees, and then looked around anxiously. If she let go, and he couldn't hold her, they might both fall outwards, over the rail.

I ran along the balcony. Something was wrong, I couldn't get enough breath. But I reached him.

'If we take one leg each—' I gasped. 'And hold the railing with the other hand—'

'You must let go,' Danu said to the girl. 'Listen! Let go with your hands. We will hold you.'

She stopped screaming. She looked down, and saw my face – the face of an enemy. Her whole body seemed to freeze in terror.

I said, 'Just let go. I won't drop you! I promise!'

I don't know if she believed me, or if she simply couldn't hold on any longer. But suddenly she was falling, and we took her weight between us, and lurched back from the edge. All three of us collapsed against the wall.

It felt like a giant hand was squeezing my lungs. I saw there were beads of sweat on Danu's face. It wasn't that long since he'd come out of hospital, I remembered. And even less time since I had, and it was this girl's family who had put us there.

In that moment, I didn't hate her, though. I didn't hate anyone. I was just glad we were safe.

19

Battlefield

The balcony shook slightly. Looking down – only for an instant because it made me feel dizzy – I saw two firefighters climbing up the ladder. I wanted to call out, but I hardly had enough breath to whisper.

Suddenly I remembered the inhaler which the doctor had given me. I dug it out of my jeans pocket and puffed at it a couple of times. Almost at once the tightness in my lungs seemed to loosen.

On the upper balcony, I could hear someone banging on a door. It was the other twin, yelling her head off.

'Mum. Are you there? Mum! Come on, wake up! Let me in, you old—'

I heard the door creaking open. A slurred, rather drunken voice said, 'What's all the noise about?'

'Mum, there's a gas leak! You gotta get out. And Tiff nearly fell off the fire escape.'

Her mother groaned. 'Is there no chance of a peaceful sleep around here?'

I sat still, breathing slowly. My thoughts were all mixed up. I had just been helping my enemies – doing good to those who hated me… loving them, even.

It was weird to realise that you can love people even if you don't like them. And strangely enough, I didn't hate them now – not as much as I used to. But if I was honest, I hadn't climbed up here to help Tiffany. I'd done it for Danu's sake, and no one else's.

He looked at me. 'I am very glad you were here,' he said. 'Without you…'

He didn't finish his sentence. He just took my hand and held it tight.

***

Soon we were safely on the ground again. One firefighter guided our twin, Tiffany, down the ladder, and I followed with Danu. When we got to the ground, Emma ran over to us and gave me a big hug. The fireman told Tiffany that her mum and sister were to go out through the front door of the flat. The men clearly didn't fancy trying to get Jackie down the fire escape.

'They won't get blown up, will they?' Tiffany asked anxiously.

'Not right now, they won't,' the fireman said. 'The gas is all turned off throughout the building, while the gas people try to mend the leak. But it's as well to be out of the way when they turn it back on again to test it.'

'Hurry up, Mum!' Tiffany shouted up at the dark building. Strange how a useless mother like Jackie could still be loved by her kids.

'Come on, let's go round and meet your mum on Hill Street,' said the fireman.

'Is it all right if we go out the other way?' I asked. 'To Canal Street?'

'Aren't you with the girl?' he said, surprised.

Emma said, 'No, we were just passing, when we heard her screaming.'

'OK, go out that way,' he said. 'But make sure you get well clear of the building. And don't hang about.'

If we'd expected any thanks from Tiffany for rescuing her, we would have been disappointed. She shot off towards Hill Street, and the fireman hurried after her.

We went on through the car park. When we got round to the Canal Street side of the Court there was another fire engine and two more policemen on guard in the street. They shouted at us to come away from the building.

I had time for a quick glance under the archway into the courtyard. Jackie O'Farrell and her daughter were being escorted out of the far exit. It didn't look as if Jackie wanted to go, but she didn't have much chance against a fireman, a police officer and Chelsea.

Then, as I looked, someone appeared under the archway. He was just a dark silhouette, coming slowly towards us. When he stepped out into the glare of the street lights, I saw that it was Kwami.

The policeman was shouting at us again. 'Are you all deaf or something? Get away from the building!'

As we went out onto the road, I said, 'Kwami! What were you doing in there? There's a gas leak. The whole building is supposed to be evacuated.'

'Oh, is that what all the noise was about?'

His eyes looked strange, sort of unfocussed. I wondered if he had discovered a secret stash of drugs. If he had tried anything like that, Dad would murder him.

'Where were you?' I demanded.

'None of your business.'

'You went looking for Paul, but you didn't find him,' I guessed. 'Know why? Because he's been arrested.'

The news didn't seem to surprise him – or please him, either. 'What's the point of that? They'll let him go again. Like the last time,' he said.

His words were definitely slurred. And he was swaying slightly.

'Are you all right?' asked Emma.

'I'm OK. Fell down, that's all. Got a knock on the head.' He put his hand up to his head in a vague sort of way, as if he wasn't quite sure where the top of his head was. I saw there was blood on his hand.

I said, 'Kwami! If you've hurt yourself, we ought to go to the hospital and get you checked over. That's what Mum would say, I know she would.'

'No! No, I'm OK. Leave me alone. I'm going home.'

Perhaps that was the best thing to do – get him back to Andrews House. Surely Mum and Dad would be there by now. They could decide what to do with him.

If we could have cut through Victory Court, we could have been there in five minutes. But we would have to go round the long way, down Canal Street, past the shops, and back up Hill Street.

Danu tried to take Kwami's arm, but Kwami shook him off. He clearly hadn't forgiven Danu for refusing to go with him earlier. But he allowed me to take one of his arms and Emma the other one. He needed our help. As we walked on, he leaned his weight on us like a wounded soldier being rescued from a battlefield.

By now I was seriously worried. 'What happened, Kwami? Did you get in a fight?'

'Yeah.'

'Who with? Robbie O'Farrell?'

He didn't answer. His weight on my shoulder was growing heavier. I could see there wasn't much chance of getting him all the way back to Andrews House – not like this.

Up ahead was a bus shelter with a bench seat. 'Can we sit down for a minute?' I said.

Kwami sank down onto the bench, groaning. He put his head in his hands. Danu said, 'He is ill. We should call for an ambulance.'

This time, Kwami didn't argue. Emma got her mobile out and called 999.

Oh, God, please let them come quickly! Please let Kwami be all right!

It was still raining. Car lights sped past without stopping, and spray from the gutter soaked my legs. No one stopped to ask if we needed help. Everyone ignored us.

And I felt as if God was ignoring us too. I was angry now. What's the good of all those promises in the Bible? Where are you now, God, when I need you?

Then a thought came into my mind. What about Robbie O'Farrell? What's happened to him?

I didn't want to think about Robbie. All my attention was on my brother. But the thought returned, like someone tugging at my sleeve. And with it came a memory of a verse from the Bible. Not one of the comforting promises – more of a warning.

But if you don't forgive others, your Father will not forgive your sins. All right then, I forgive him. I forgive Robbie O'Farrell, and Paul, and the whole lot of them. Now will you listen to me, Lord? Now will the ambulance come… please?

Forgiveness is more than just words.

I suddenly knew that I had to find out what had happened to Robbie.

'Kwami,' I said, 'tell me. Did you have a fight with Robbie?'

Kwami muttered something I couldn't hear.

'You didn't kill him, did you?'

'I don't know.'

'What do you mean, you don't know?'

He turned to look at me. He spoke in Zansi so that the others wouldn't understand. 'I looked for him in that den of his. In the basement, in the dark. He was asleep – I heard him snoring. But he must have heard me climbing up the pipes. When I got to the top, he pulled a knife on me.'

He held out his hand. I could see a thin line of dried blood across his fingers.

'Oh, Kwami…'

'But I had a knife too. I cut him and he yelled. And then the den began to break up, and I fell onto the floor. I banged my head; must have knocked myself out.'

I stared at him. 'So is Robbie… still there?'

'I don't know. I didn't stay around to look. I just got out.'

'But what if you killed him? Or hurt him so bad he could bleed to death?'

'Best thing that could happen,' Kwami muttered. 'If he's dead, he can't tell anyone.'

Oh, God! What a mess! What do we do now?

The easiest thing would be what Kwami had done – just walk away. Try to forget the whole thing. Hope that Robbie was dead, and no one would ever know who did it. But I would know, and so would Kwami. The guilty secret would always be there, dark and silent, like a crocodile hiding in a river.

What if Robbie was still alive? Too badly hurt to get out – lying there alone in the dark, in an empty building, no one to hear him if he shouted. And then, if the men turned the gas on and something went wrong...

Forgiveness is more than just words. It means treating your enemy like your brother.

'I've got to go back to Victory Court,' I said to Emma and Danu. 'I won't be long. Look after Kwami for me.'

'But why? What—'

I didn't waste time explaining. Kwami might try to stop me doing what I knew was right. Danu looked concerned, but I just took off, hurrying back the way we had come. It wasn't far, but by the time I got back to the Court, I could hardly get my words out.

'There may be someone still in there,' I gasped to the policemen on guard. 'He's in the basement. Maybe he's hurt, or… unconscious.'

Or dead. But I didn't want to think about that.

He spoke quickly on his intercom. 'Hold everything. I've been told there may be someone still in the building.' Then he asked me where.

'The basement – through a door there, and down some steps. This guy Robbie had like a den in the far corner, high up; behind the boiler. But he might have fallen down… hurt himself… I don't know.'

'All right. We'll take a look.' He shouted to a couple of firefighters.

I wanted to stay around to see what happened. But I also wanted to get back to Kwami. I started walking back to the bus stop – walking, not running. I was dreading what Kwami might say when he found out what I'd done.

If Robbie was still alive – if I had saved his life – would it mean that I'd got Kwami into trouble? But perhaps Robbie wouldn't be able to say who had attacked him. After all it had been dark, he'd been half-asleep, and he had lots of other enemies besides my family.

Kwami would still think I shouldn't have done it, though. He believed in an eye for an eye, a tooth for a tooth, on and on, year after year… I didn't want to live like that.

You are right, God. I'm sorry I held onto my feelings of hate, instead of loving my enemies, forgiving them… Please teach me to live the way you want me to.

You are already learning.

For the first time in days, I felt the nearness of God, and the warmth of his love, wrapping me round like a great, thick coat. Like the loving arms of a father, always ready to welcome his children home.

***

As I got back to the others, an ambulance was just pulling up. The paramedics got Kwami inside and started checking him over. Emma, Danu and I had to wait outside.

A couple of minutes later, we heard the siren of another ambulance. 'Oh, great,' said Emma. 'Like buses. You wait ages, and then two come at once.'

But this one didn't stop for us. And I had seen where it came from – out of Victory Court. Was Robbie on board? If so, then to judge by the way it was racing along, he must still be alive…

As it vanished in the distance, the driver of our ambulance called me over. 'We're going to take your brother to hospital for some further checks,' he said.

'Oh. Is he going to be OK?'

'It's possible he has concussion. He needs—'

But I never heard what Kwami needed.

Without any warning, the dark sky turned white. The air trembled, and a huge sound, too loud to hear, boomed in my ears. And the pavement shook.

I found I was crouching on the ground, covering my face. Bricks and debris rained down like hailstones on the bus shelter roof. It felt like a volcano erupting, or the end of the world.

There was broken glass on the pavement. Someone was screaming. A terrified dog ran down the road, barking madly.

'Looks like they didn't manage to fix that gas leak,' the ambulance driver said.

20

Shock waves

It was the big news story on Christmas Day. It was the first story on every TV news report. When you saw the damage to Victory Court, you could hardly believe that no one had died in the explosion. Two gasmen had been injured, and 150 people were now homeless. But it could easily have been so much worse.

Gas had been leaking from a pipe near our flat, probably damaged by the fire. It had travelled upwards into the roof space above the top floor flats. This could have been happening for days. No one had smelt it, because our flat, like the ones above and beside it, was empty.

When it finally ignited, it blew the roof off the western side of the Court. The top floor flats were left open to the sky, like a ruined castle. If anyone had been inside them at the time, they would have been killed.

The shock waves from the explosion made both the entrance arches collapse. The floors above simply fell into the gap. The basement, where Robbie had been, was buried under tons of rubble. If they hadn't got him out in time, he would certainly have been killed, and his body wouldn't have been found for weeks.

As it was, he had survived. We heard this from Mrs Hoskins, a few days later. We had all come to the community centre, to a Council-run meeting about Victory Court.

Mrs Hoskins told me that Robbie was in hospital – he'd been stabbed in the stomach, but he was on the mend. No one seemed to know who did it. When she said this, she looked hard at Kwami, but he managed not to react. (He had been in hospital too, but only for a few hours. He was fine, except for that thin knife scar across his fingers.)

Robbie's mother was at the meeting, and for once, she seemed to be stone cold sober. The twins were with her, looking restless and bored. Tiffany caught my eye once and instantly looked away.

I wondered where the O'Farrells were living now, and whether they'd made enemies yet. Everyone had been moved out of the Court – some to stay with friends or relatives, others to temporary accommodation all across the city. Victory Court was going to be demolished. It would be redesigned and rebuilt – bigger, better and safer.

'How long is that going to take?' someone asked the man from the Council.

'Two to three years, we estimate.'

A gasp of horror went around the audience.

'You can't expect us to live like pigs, four to a room, for three years!' Jackie O'Farrell shouted. 'It's a disgrace!'

'You can thank your son for it,' shouted an anonymous voice from the back. 'It's all his fault.'

Yes, if Paul hadn't set fire to our flat... but then again, if John hadn't destroyed the motorbike... if Paul hadn't tried to run us over... if only, if only...

But you can't turn back time. You can only start again from where you are, and try to do better from now on.

The Council man banged on the table and shouted for silence. He said, 'I can promise you, no one will have to live in temporary accommodation for three years. We will rehouse you all as top priority, whenever places become available.'

No one believed that this promise meant much. People muttered to themselves.

But then someone asked a question about the Victory Fund. This was a charity set up by the *Daily Messenger*, to help the residents of the Court. Some families had lost everything and hadn't even been insured.

A woman from the *Messenger* stood up and announced that the fund had raised almost £1,000,000, with more money still coming in. (People must have been generous because it was Christmas – good timing, Paul.) She started handing out forms so that people could fill in their details.

'You can almost see the pound signs lighting up in some people's eyes,' said John. 'They're going to claim for things they never owned in the first place.'

'What, you mean the O'Farrells never owned a home cinema system and a sauna and a brand new fitted kitchen?' said Kwami.

The meeting ended with everyone in a better mood. As we left the building, we were only a few feet away from the O'Farrells. I saw Tiffany tug at her mother's sleeve. She was pointing at me.

'That's her. She helped to rescue me.'

'Yeah, she's the one,' said Chelsea.

Their mother looked at me, surprised. Her glance flickered over the rest of my family, then back to me. 'I never knew it was you,' she said. 'Thanks. I won't forget this.'

I won't forget this... Coming from Paul, it would have been a threat. From Jackie it was more like an offer of peace.

'That's OK,' was all I could think of to say.

We went our separate ways. I haven't seen her since.

***

In one way, we're lucky. Months ago, Mum put our name on the list for some new flats being built in the grounds of her hospital. They were for hospital workers and their families. At that stage, because we already had a flat, we hadn't much chance of getting one. But now we're high priority – top of the queue.

So when the flats are ready, in another few weeks, we'll be moving in. Goodbye forever to Victory Court! Hello to a modern building, with lifts instead of stinking stairwells, and clean corridors instead of rubbish-strewn balconies. I can't wait.

There's only one disadvantage – I'll be further away from where Danu lives.

I sort of guessed he was going to ask me out. All the same, when he did, I couldn't speak for a few seconds. He looked at me anxiously – and then I said yes, and he smiled that smile of his.

One problem... I would have to tell my family. I really wasn't sure what Dad would say. When I told Charlie and Emma about this, they didn't understand at first. But Emma reminded Charlie of the play we'd been reading in school – *Romeo and Juliet*.

'It's just like the Montagues and the Capulets,' she said. 'They were enemies, but their children fell in love – romantic, or what?'

Charlie said, 'You mean Danu and Abena are Romeo and Juliet? I hope not.'

'Right,' I said. 'We're not planning to get married in secret and then kill ourselves.'

I took things gradually. I brought Danu round to meet my family on Sunday afternoon. Dad and Mum were interested to meet the boy whose life we'd helped to save. And they liked him, I could tell.

Later, when I told them he had asked me out, they both looked worried.

'I am not going to say don't go out with him,' Dad said. 'But if you marry him, you won't find life easy if you go back to Mazundi.'

'Dad! You're thinking way too far ahead. He's asked me out, that's all. And anyway, he may not be here for long. If things in Mazundi settle down, his family are going back there.'

Actually, in the last few days, the news from Mazundi has been good. That is, there's been no mention of it on TV (no news is good news), and my cousins say that things seem to be more peaceful. The Government generals are having talks with the leader of the rebel army. This would never have happened if

President Baretse was still in power. He would have made his soldiers fight on to the bitter end.

I don't know what will happen. Maybe the peace talks will be able to find a solution to Mazundi's problems; maybe not. 'Keep on praying,' Mum says.

***

When the time seemed right, I told Kwami what I had done on the night of the explosion. I was afraid he would be mad at me – and he was.

'You shouldn't have said anything!' he shouted. 'What if Robbie told the police it was me?'

'If he was going to do that, you would have been arrested by now,' I said.

'How do you know? Maybe he doesn't remember. Maybe it will come back to him as he gets better.'

I saw Kwami was frightened as well as angry. Fear hung over him like a dark, threatening cloud – the fear of being found out.

There was one way to get rid of the fear, and that was to own up to what he'd done and take the punishment. But I didn't think he would be brave enough to do that. He'd rather go on living under the dark cloud, unsure of what would happen... hoping he was safe, but never knowing for certain.

'You should be glad Robbie didn't die,' I told him. 'Would you want to have it on your conscience for the rest of your life – killing someone?'

'No,' he admitted. 'Not even a low-life like Robbie.'

I said, 'You still hate him, don't you?'

'I hate the whole lot of them! I hope they get rehoused on the 15th floor of a cockroach-infested tower block where the lifts don't work! I hope Paul goes to prison for years!' (Paul is still in prison, waiting to go on trial for arson.)

When Kwami talks like this, I can see that Danu's father was right – hatred can burn people up inside. And it can sort of imprison us, locked in with thoughts of the past. It's better to forgive, and walk away free.

And when we forgive other people, God can forgive us. Simple as that.

***

On Sunday night at youth group, Mark announced the grand total raised by the Market Square sleepout – over £20,000. (Of course, that wasn't just down to us. But still, pretty impressive money for one night's work, or rather sleep.)

He was keen to take on another *Help-the-Homeless* type of project, and he asked for ideas. Someone suggested doing something to help the ex-residents of Victory Court.

'Like what?' asked Mark. 'Come on, people, ideas, please.'

'Something for the kids,' I suggested. 'I mean, there are lots of them living in temporary places, whole families crammed into one or two rooms. I know my brother gets really fed up.'

There were lots of suggestions.

'Maybe we could give a party.'

'Or start a kids' club on a Saturday.'

'Take them out somewhere. Like to a theme park.'

'Great idea,' said Mark. 'I'll see if I can get a list of names, and we'll start organising it.'

Uh-oh! I suddenly remembered two names which were bound to be on the list: Tiffany and Chelsea O'Farrell.

'Some of these kids may be a bit hard to handle,' I said. 'You know – trouble-makers.' But no one was listening.

So look out. If you see a headline, *Seven-year-old twins cause chaos at theme park*, you'll know exactly who to blame.